VEXED ON A VISIT

Vexed on a Visit

(A Lacey Doyle Cozy Mystery—Book 4)

Fiona Grace

FIONA GRACE

Debut author Fiona Grace is author of the LACEY DOYLE COZY MYSTERY series, comprising nine books (and counting); of the TUSCAN VINEYARD COZY MYSTERY series, comprising three books (and counting); of the DUBIOUS WITCH COZY MYSTERY series, comprising three books (and counting); and of the BEACHFRONT BAKERY COZY MYSTERY series, comprising three books (and counting).

MURDER IN THE MANOR (A Lacey Doyle Cozy Mystery—Book 1) is available as a free download on Amazon!

Fiona would love to hear from you, so please visit www.fionagraceauthor.com to receive free ebooks, hear the latest news, and stay in touch.

TABLE OF CONTENTS

CHAPTER ONE

"How's it going up there?" Lacey called fretfully, peering up the metal rungs of the ladder at Gina's feet.

The two women were in Lacey's antiques store, displaying a bunch of ugly marionettes Gina had found in the storeroom and insisted would "sell like hot cakes." And, despite being twenty-odd years Lacey's senior, Gina had also taken it upon herself to climb the ladder into the recesses between the ceiling beams to hang them.

"I'm sixty-five years young, missy," she called down to Lacey, who'd been left helplessly at the bottom, holding the ladder. "I'm not a frail old lady yet."

Suddenly, a creepy wooden marionette bounced down on its strings, making Lacey start. The grotesque-looking man had a hooked nose and jester's hat, and he dangled above Lacey's head, grinning evilly. She shuddered, silently questioning Gina's judgment. Who on earth would want to buy such an unpleasant-looking thing?

"So?" came Gina's trilling voice from the top of the ladder. "Have you worked out where Tom is taking you for your romantic getaway yet?"

Lacey's cheeks warmed at the mention of her beau. Tom had recently announced he was taking her on a romantic trip, and had been sending her photographic clues every day since as to the location. The last image had been of a craggy white cliff with a gorgeous blue sky behind it.

"Somewhere by the sea," Lacey replied dreamily.

Wherever it was, it looked absolutely idyllic. But it could be the most desolate place on earth as far as Lacey was concerned, and she'd still be thrilled for the break. To say she was overdue some time off was an understatement. Ever since she'd opened her antiques store in the seaside town of Wilfordshire, England, the only time she'd had so much as two consecutive days off had been when she was investigating gruesome murders. That didn't really count as a break, as far as Lacey was concerned!

Just then, another marionette bounced down on its strings above Lacey's head, snapping her out of her daydream. This one depicted a portly scullery maid, with a bonnet and apron. She had the same grotesque face as the first. Lacey scrunched her nose with displeasure.

"Whose idea was it to suspend these horrible things from the ceiling again?" she said. "I don't know how much I'm going to like them peering down at me all day."

From above, Gina cackled. "I promise you they'll sell quickly. Punch and Judy puppets are an institution here in England. I can't believe you've had them hidden away in a box for so long! At least we got them out in time for the summer crowds."

Lacey couldn't understand the appeal of the ugly puppets, but she trusted Gina on this one. As a born and bred New Yorker, the oddities of English culture often went right over Lacey's head.

"So, what were the other clues?" Gina called down. "I want to get to the bottom of this mystery!"

Holding onto the ladder with one hand, Lacey used the other to scoop her cell phone from her jeans pocket. She scrolled through the images with her thumb.

"A castle," she called up. "A bird ... maybe a bluebird? A *sandwich*! A black-and-white photo of a lady holding one of those 1940s-style microphones. And a Roman emperor."

"A Roman emperor?" Gina repeated, surprised. "Maybe he's taking you to Italy!"

"Italy? It's not exactly famed for its sandwiches, is it?" Lacey quipped, before another marionette fell into place and wiped the smirk right off her face. This one was a creepy clown with lurid orange curls. Its cracked paint work made it look even more sinister. She shuddered.

"Careful with that sarcasm, young lady," Gina trilled down. "I see our British humor is rubbing off on you."

"It's a staycation, anyway," Lacey continued. "So it'll be somewhere in Eng—ah!"

Gina had released yet another one of her marionettes, only this one had smacked Lacey right on her head. She batted it away and found herself staring into the face of a police officer, grinning threateningly and holding a truncheon in its silly puppet hand. She immediately thought of Superintendent Turner of the Wilfordshire Police Department, a man she certainly hoped she'd have no dealings with again any time soon.

"How many of these nasty things do you have up there?" Lacey cried, rubbing her sore head.

"That's the last of them," Gina called down brightly, none the wiser. The ladder squeaked under her weight as she reversed down it. When she safely reached the bottom, she faced Lacey. "You don't have the dog puppet, unfortunately, and the string of sausages fell off."

She held up the pretend sausages. Lacey didn't even want to know what that was all about.

"Show me these piccies then," Gina said, craning her head to peer upside down at the image on Lacey's cell phone screen.

Lacey thumbed through them.

"Oh!" Gina suddenly exclaimed. "Why didn't you tell me they were *white* cliffs? Darling, you're going to Dover!"

And with that, she launched into song. Her shrill, high-pitched voice echoed through the entire store, right up into the ceiling beams. Lacey scrunched her face into a wince.

"*There'll be bluebirds over*—the irony of course being that bluebirds aren't native to England," she added as a hurried aside before launching into the next line of the song, "—*the white cliffs of Dover.*" She resumed speaking. "You must know the song? It's an old wartime classic."

"I know the song," Lacey said. Then she clicked her fingers. "The black-and-white photo of the singer with the old microphone!" She scrolled to the picture and showed it to Gina.

"Oh yes. That's Vera Lynn, all right," Gina confirmed with a nod.

The bluebirds. The cliffs. The Roman emperor.

"Tom's taking me to Dover," Lacey said with breathless wonder.

"How charming," Gina gushed, giving Lacey a playful poke in the ribs.

A ripple of excitement peeled through Lacey's whole body. She'd been happy enough about the secret romantic getaway as it was. Then Tom started sending his trail of bread crumb clues, and she'd grown increasingly excited. Now that she'd worked out where she was actually going, she was utterly delighted.

She quickly texted Tom, *"Got it!"* and glanced through the window of her store into his patisserie opposite, watching him check his phone and begin to laugh.

But just as Lacey was gazing at her beau through the window, a sudden figure moved into her line of sight, spoiling her view. As she realized who it was staring at her, the excitement she'd been feeling just moments earlier seeped out of her all in one go, like a candle being extinguished. It was replaced instead by an ominous feeling of dread. Taryn.

The boutique owner from the store next door was always meddling in Lacey's life, trying to drive her out of town. Why she had such a vendetta against her, Lacey had never quite gotten to the bottom of, beyond the obvious fact she'd briefly dated Tom many moons ago. It was more likely because she was jealous of her success, or because she was prejudiced toward an American blighting the otherwise perfectly British high street. It was probably a bit of both.

The store bell jangled angrily as Taryn barged her way inside and charged across the floorboards in black stilettos and her customary LBD. Her sharp, bony shoulders were on full display.

"Oh look, it's the Grim Reaper," Gina murmured under her breath, as the two women watched Taryn give a wide berth around the collection of ugly marionettes, pulling a disgusted face and almost stepping on Chester, the dog. The English Shepherd let out a little whine of distress at the sudden intrusion on his slumbering. Then he dropped his head and covered it with his paws, something Lacey would do as well if social convention allowed it.

The scowling woman halted abruptly in front of Lacey and Gina.

"How can I help you, Taryn?" Lacey asked thinly, with wry expectation.

"Are you aware," Taryn began haughtily, "that a PIGEON has made a NEST above your door? Its constant twittering is driving me mad! You need to call an exterminator. NOW."

"Firstly, she's not a pigeon," Lacey retorted.

"Her name is Martina," Gina added, with mock offense.

Taryn's stony glare went from one woman to the other. She folded her arms. "You named a pigeon?"

"I told you," Lacey said. "She's not a pigeon. She's a house martin."

"And Martina is a fine and fitting name for a house martin," Gina said, nodding along with Lacey.

"She's flown all the way from Africa to raise her babies above my store's porch," Lacey added.

"And we're both honored to have her here," Gina finished, rounding off their comedy double-act.

Lacey could hardly hold back her laughter.

Taryn looked furious. Her nostrils flared. "If you don't get rid of *it*, I'll call an exterminator myself," she threatened between her teeth.

Gina scoffed. "I think you'll find there's no such thing, my dear. No one will move a nest during breeding season!"

Taryn looked like she was about to blow a blood vessel. "When does breeding season end?" she asked through gritted teeth.

"November. Ish," Gina said.

Taryn clenched down on her jaw furiously. "Typical!" she bellowed, before spinning on her heel and storming right into the marionettes. She screamed and batted them out of her face. With a final glare over her shoulder at Lacey and Gina, she stormed out the way she'd come.

The moment she was gone, Lacey and Gina burst into laughter. Lacey laughed so hard, tears started to roll down her cheeks.

"Never a dull moment," she said through her dying chuckles, wiping the tears away. But then she paused. "Hold on a minute. Chester didn't growl at Taryn."

Normally, her English Shepherd would emit a low grumble the entire time Taryn was in his line of sight. Since he came with the store, he'd actually known Taryn far longer than Lacey and there was more bad blood between the two of them than between Taryn and Lacey! Chester treated Taryn like she was his very own Cruella De Vil.

"Maybe he doesn't mind her now?" Gina suggested, dabbing her sleeve beneath her bright red glasses to remove her own tears.

Lacey looked unconvinced. "I highly doubt that. I mean, she literally almost just stepped on him! No, it's something else."

She hurried over to Chester and gently moved his paws off his head. He barely seemed to notice, so Lacey lifted his head up from beneath his chin. It felt heavy, like he was too weak to lift it himself. When their eyes met, Lacey saw his were watery and a little bloodshot. He let out a soft whine.

"Oh, darling," Lacey said, her heart skipping several beats. "Are you sick?"

Chester whined as if in confirmation, and Lacey's stomach clenched with worry.

"Gina, I'd better get him to the vet," she said hurriedly, looking over at her friend. "Will you be okay to mind the shop?"

"Of course," Gina said, waving her concerns off with a hand. "I always am."

Lacey clipped on Chester's leash and coaxed him out of the store, her mind frantic with worry for her poor, sick pup.

Chapter Two

"Chester!" the receptionist called.

Lacey had spent a short but anxiety-provoking wait in the reception room of Wilfordshire's finest veterinary practice, having raced Chester through the winding cobblestone streets in her rusty secondhand car.

She stood from the uncomfortable plastic reception room chair and gave Chester's leash a little tug. He let out an angry huff—extremely out of character, Lacey noted anxiously—and slowly plodded after her into the treatment room.

The vet, Lakshmi, looked up as they entered. She was a short Asian woman, completely swamped by her dark green scrubs. Her childlike features made her look far too young to have completed the years of education her profession demanded.

"Oh dear," she exclaimed, after taking just one look at Chester's lumbering figure. "What's the matter here?"

Lacey gulped with apprehension as Chester leapt dutifully up onto the examination table. "He's not himself," she explained. "He seems lethargic. Like he's lost his usual spark."

Lakshmi began to check him over, placing a thermometer in his ear, shining a miniature torch in his eyes. Chester obliged, either comfortable enough with Lakshmi to allow it, or too tired from whatever was ailing him to resist.

"I think someone's suffering from a case of canine influenza," Lakshmi said, clicking off her torch and returning it to her breast pocket. "Do you have any other pets at home?"

"Not at home, but he spends almost every day with his best friend, Boudica," Lacey explained, before hastily clarifying, "who's also a dog."

"Well, in that case, it might be a good idea to keep him here in order to stop him from infecting her. I can keep him under close observation, and prescribe him some water pills to prevent dehydration."

Lacey felt her heart break in two. Her poor pup!

"But I've never gone a night without him since I got him," she said, mournfully.

Lakshmi's features softened in understanding. "You can come and visit him whenever you want. In fact, I'd encourage it. Seeing a familiar face can really help reduce their stress levels."

Lacey bit down on her lip. The thought of Chester locked in one of the kennels out back, all alone and confused, was making it start to tremble. "How long will he need to stay in?" she asked.

"Canine flu is a bit like human flu," Lakshmi explained. "So it could be up to two weeks."

"Two weeks!" Lacey exclaimed. She could feel her grief lodged in her throat.

"I know it will be hard," Lakshmi said kindly. "But it's for the best. He'll be in good hands. Do you want to go ahead and admit him?" She held out a clipboard, upon which was a pink form of admittance, and gave it an expectant nudge toward Lacey.

Despite the agonizing ache in her chest, Lacey grabbed the pen and signed on the dotted line. Then she bent her face into the ruff of Chester's neck, letting her tears discreetly fall into his fur.

"You'll be okay, boy," she murmured.

Chester whined sadly.

Then Lacey straightened up and hurried out of the vet's office before she broke down fully. It wasn't until she was safely in her car that she allowed her tears to flow freely.

Chester had been by her side every single day since she'd moved to Wilfordshire. He was her shadow. Her other half. Her partner in crime. No, her sidekick in *solving* crime. How was she going to cope for two whole weeks without his comforting presence beside her?

"Oh no!" Lacey suddenly exclaimed, with a gasp. She was supposed to be leaving in two days for her secret getaway with Tom. There was no way she'd be able to go now. Lakshmi had said frequent visits from a familiar face would help Chester cope with the stress. She couldn't leave him in his time of need.

She was bitterly disappointed; she'd really been looking forward to a romantic break with Tom.

With a deep sigh of sadness, Lacey fetched her cell phone from her purse so she could call him and break the news. But before she got the chance, she noticed a message had come in from Xavier Santino.

She hesitated, twisting her lips in consternation. The Spanish man was a contact of Lacey's from the antiques world. He claimed to have met her missing father, Francis. But just when Lacey had decided he had ulterior, romantic motives for being in contact with her, and suggested they cool off their communication, Xavier had responded by claiming he knew where Francis was. Lacey had deliberated for hours over whether to reply or not. She couldn't be certain he wasn't just using her father as bait to reel her in. In the end, the lure had proved too hard to resist. The mystery of her father's disappearance was like a huge black cloud that hung over her everywhere she went. Any lead felt like a lifeline, even if she was potentially inviting trouble into her life. And so she'd reinstated contact with Xavier, who'd given her the next cryptic piece of the puzzle: Canterbury. Her father had apparently, and fairly recently, been spotted in the English town of Canterbury . . .

She had not known how to process that. For years, she'd run through a hundred different scenarios in her mind. Sometimes, she took comfort in the idea that he'd passed away shortly after leaving the family inexplicably, and that he'd never really chosen to go, or perhaps was even heading home when it happened. Then just as soon as she'd made peace with the idea he was dead, her mind would switch lanes and instead tell her that he'd chosen to run away because he couldn't stand his wife, Shirley, and his children, her and Naomi. The truth was that while no answer would ever be satisfactory, any answer would be better than none.

Before opening Xavier's message, Lacey tried to remember what question of hers had prompted it. *How recently?* Yes, that was the last message she'd sent him. Because there was a big difference between a year-old sighting and a decade-old sighting, even though both would send her into a tailspin from which she wasn't sure she'd ever recover.

She braced herself and tapped the little envelope symbol. The words: *I do not know* filled the screen. Lacey felt deflated. It seemed as if Xavier had been leading her on after all.

Bitter with disappointment, Lacey exited out of the screen, only to see there'd been a flurry of activity on the messaging app she shared with her mom and younger sister. A dozen or so bright red exclamation point alerts flashed at Lacey, demanding attention. Her mom and sister were known for melodrama, but that didn't stop Lacey from instantly fearing the worst.

She opened up the messaging app and saw all the alerts belonged to Naomi. She appeared to have sent a barrage of questions. Very strange questions...

How close is Wilfordshire to Scotland?

Does England have a monsoon season?

Do you get mosquitoes in the summer?

Lacey narrowed her eyes, the lashes still tacky with tears. She was utterly perplexed. Why was Naomi taking such a strange and sudden interest in the United Kingdom?

She typed back:

Scotland is 500 miles away.

There are no monsoons, but it does rain a lot.

Yes, there are mosquitoes.

Then she finally added,

Is everything okay?

Naomi's reply was immediate. It was as if her younger sister had literally been staring at her phone waiting for Lacey to answer her bizarre list of questions.

Are there mountains in Wilfordshire?

Lacey threw her hands up in frustration. What on earth was Naomi going on about? Why the sudden curiosity?

No, Lacey replied. *There are cliffs. Why are you asking?*

Lacey couldn't help but wonder if Naomi had discovered some kind of lead on their father—a photo on a rainy mountain, for example—but that was probably wishful thinking on her part. Naomi preferred to pretend their dad had never existed. It was far more likely that her sister was in a pub quiz.

Her phone continued to beep and buzz as yet more strange questions came in from Naomi. Lacey sighed and put her phone away. It had been a brief distraction from her grief over Chester but she couldn't sit here in the veterinarian's parking lot all day; she had a store to run.

Lacey drove back to the store and entered.

Gina took one look at her tear-stained face and exclaimed, "Chester's been put down!"

"No!" Lacey refuted. "He's sick. He has to stay at the vet's for a while to be observed."

Gina pressed a hand to her chest. "Thank goodness. You scared me."

Lacey slumped at the desk, sinking her head into her hands. It was only then that she realized Naomi's messages had distracted her completely from calling Tom and canceling the Dover trip. She looked out through the window across the street to the patisserie, watching as he moved deftly through his store, and smiled sadly. She'd be so looking forward to spending a romantic getaway with him.

"I'll have to cancel the trip to Dover now," Lacey said through a long sigh. "I can't leave Chester while he's sick. Lakshmi said he'd benefit from a visitor."

"I can visit him," Gina told her.

Lacey paused. She raised her head to meet Gina's gaze. Then she shook it. "I couldn't ask you to do that. You already do so much."

"Exactly. What's another chore to add to the list?"

Lacey was reticent. She sometimes felt like she put too many demands on Gina's shoulders. She balked at the idea of becoming the sort of boss who expected her employees to behave like PAs, just as her fierce old boss in New York had.

Lacey shook her head. "No. It wouldn't be fair. You can't run the store and care for Boudica *and* check in on Chester every day."

"And you can't keep working day after day without a break," her friend contested. She put her hands on her hips and glared at her sternly. "When was the last time you took a day off?"

Lacey started calculating it back in her mind, but Gina stopped her before she reached the answer.

"Exactly!" Gina exclaimed. "You can't even remember it was so long ago! Look, missy, I'm ordering you to go on your trip. If you don't go, I'll quit."

Lacey felt her lips begin to twitch upward. Where would she be without Gina? "I'll get you a thank you gift," she said meekly.

"No need!" Gina bellowed with flourish. "Your gift can be coming back relaxed and happy."

"I have been pretty tense recently, haven't I?" Lacey said.

Gina nodded emphatically.

A lot had happened since her move to England, Lacey reasoned. Though most of it had been positive, the good had been mixed in with a whole lot of negative. All had left their mark on her. Lacey needed to press the reset button, to clear the cobwebs out of her mind.

"If you really don't mind," Lacey said.

Gina put her hand on her heart. "I honestly, one hundred percent, do not mind."

Lacey felt a surge of elation. She leapt up from her seat, beckoning to Gina over the counter to hug her. But before she got the chance, the bell over the door rang, heralding in some customers. Very loud American voices filled the store.

Very loud, very familiar American voices…

Lacey's head darted to the door. Bustling in through the entrance of her antiques store were none other than her sister, Naomi, her nephew, Frankie…and her mother.

CHAPTER THREE

Lacey blinked. Surely she was hallucinating? But when her auburn-haired nephew screeched, "Auntie Lacey!" there was no doubt anymore. Her mother, sister, and nephew were really here! In Wilfordshire! Standing in her store!

Gina looked across to Lacey and her mouth formed a perfect surprised O. "Lacey? Is this your family?"

Her eyes were wide behind her thick red-framed spectacles. But Lacey was too stunned to reply. All she could do was stare.

How were they here? *Why* were they here?

The loud thud of Frankie dumping his backpack on the floor jerked Lacey out of her ruminations. He came charging across the store toward her.

He'd grown at least a foot since Lacey had last seen him, and was now sporting some grown-up teeth that transformed his baby face into one of a young boy.

"Surprise!" he exclaimed, as he barreled into her so hard the wind was knocked right out of her. His arms locked around her waist like a python.

"What are you guys doing here?" Lacey stammered, as she patted his ginger curls.

"Air miles," Naomi said as she heaved a very large, overstuffed suitcase over a bump in the floorboards. She was dressed fashionably in this season's patterned maxi summer dress and cut-off denim jacket, accessorized with delicate rose gold jewelry. Lacey immediately felt on edge about her casual attire; Naomi had a tendency to be highly critical of her appearance.

Coming up behind Naomi, cradling a large floral-patterned hold-all, as if ready to bolt at any second, was Shirley, Lacey's mom. The sight of her put Lacey immediately on edge.

"I racked up a ton of air miles," Shirley explained, pushing her sunglasses onto her head. "Frankie was desperate to visit Scotland so we thought we'd come see you on the way."

As the limpet that was Frankie detached himself from Lacey and started exploring the store, Lacey's eyebrows drew together with confusion. "But Scotland is a completely different country! Literally hundreds of miles in that direction." She pointed out the window, in the opposite direction of the ocean.

"We know that," Shirley countered, sounding immediately offended at Lacey's insinuation they didn't. "But it was cheaper to fly into England with a layover than to go straight there."

"We're just dropping in," Naomi added. "On our way to Edinburgh." She incorrectly pronounced it as the three-syllabled Ed-in-burg, rather than the four-syllabled Ed-in-bu-rugh as Lacey had discovered was correct.

Lacey couldn't help but feel relieved their visit was just a short one. "How long is the layover for then?" she asked.

Shirley, who was peering at a shelf of crockery, answered absent-mindedly. "Five days."

"Days? Do you mean hours?" Lacey asked.

Shirley turned her face from the display to Lacey. "No. Five days," she said simply.

All the air left Lacey's lungs in one sudden whoosh. She almost choked on her shock. Five days? FIVE DAYS? What kind of a layover took five days? How was she supposed to entertain them? And what about the long weekend in Dover with Tom? Their romantic getaway was right in the middle of her family's impromptu visit! She couldn't exactly up and leave them when they'd come all this way.

"I wasn't sure about it at first," Naomi said, taking over the story from Shirley. "Since a five-day detour during a ten-day vacation seemed a bit inconvenient. But then Mom suggested we could come here and surprise you. Much better than spending five days in an airport hotel!"

She laughed, but Lacey couldn't even raise a smile. It was better for them, sure, but it wasn't better for Lacey! All they'd done was shift the inconvenience onto Lacey's shoulders. And they were utterly clueless that their decision would have any impact on her whatsoever.

"You should've called, or checked, or something," Lacey said, panicking. "I've not had any time to prepare."

"What do you need to prepare?" Shirley asked.

"My house," Lacey said quickly. She'd actually been referring to the mental preparations she usually undertook in advance of spending time with her family, but they certainly didn't need to know that. "Where am I supposed to put you all? I only have one spare room."

"Jeez," Naomi said, glancing over from the shelving unit filled with figurines she'd been idly perusing. "We can get a hotel if we have to. Seriously, I thought you'd be more happy to see us."

"I *am* happy," Lacey said, quickly, though her tone was so shrouded in stress it sounded distinctly unconvincing. "I'm just taken aback. It's a lot to process having you suddenly here. Five minutes ago you were texting me about weather and mountains and..."

She stopped as her sister grinned and wiggled her eyebrows. It finally dawned on Lacey what Naomi's random messages had really been about. She'd been hinting at their imminent arrival! But Lacey had been so focused on the situation with Chester, she'd completely failed to notice.

Lacey burst out laughing, and the silliness of it all helped her finally overcome her shock. She went over to her mom and sister and hugged them both.

"Welcome!" she exclaimed, with the hospitality they'd probably been expecting from her in the first place.

"Is this Chester?" came Frankie's voice. He was crouching beside Boudica, petting her.

"Chester's at the vet," Lacey explained. "That's Gina's dog, Boudica."

"Boudica?" Frankie exclaimed with excitement, looking up at Gina. "Like the Celtic warrior queen?"

"Why yes, that's right!" Gina said, looking down at the small boy with an amazed look in her eyes. "How do you know that?"

Frankie pointed to his ginger curls and grinned.

"He's obsessed with anyone with ginger hair," Naomi explained, sounding very much like a mother who'd reached the end of her patience for a child's latest obsession. "He's taken it upon himself to study up on every redheaded historical figure."

"I know a bunch of British ones too," Frankie boasted. "Queen Elizabeth the first. King Henry the eighth. Ron Weasley."

Lacey chuckled. "I'm not sure Ron Weasley counts as a historical figure," she began to say, but she was interrupted by the sound of the bell over the door tinkling.

For a brief moment, Lacey was glad for the reprieve of a customer. A couple of minutes of normality might be all she needed to fully recalibrate her brain to this strange new reality. But when she saw who the tinkle was heralding in, her stomach dropped to her toes.

Tom.

What is he doing here?! Lacey thought desperately, panic setting in once more. She wasn't ready to introduce him to her mother!

These days, Tom was usually too busy to drop in and visit her during the day. The summer season brought so many tourists to Wilfordshire, and after his old assistant Lucia had left to take up a position at the Lodge B&B, Tom never seemed to have a spare second. But now, at the worst possible time, he'd come to see her!

"Morning," Tom announced as he entered, all mischievous smiles and twinkling green eyes.

"Oooh," Naomi said under her breath. The look in her eye had immediately changed to that of a predator homing in on its prey. "Hello, Mr. Hotstuff."

Of course her man-eater sister would take a shine to a handsome man like Tom.

Tom strolled right over to Lacey and planted a kiss on her cheek. Lacey froze, as if bracing for impact.

Naomi's eyes widened. Shirley's narrowed. Frankie pulled a disgusted face.

"Ewww!" he exclaimed. "Auntie Lacey has a *boyfriend*."

Tom looked at her, frowning. "Auntie?" Then his eyes widened with understanding. "Lacey, is this your family?"

Before Lacey had a chance to speak, Naomi shoved her way forward and proffered her hand to him.

"I'm Naomi, the younger, funnier sister. And you must be *Tom*." She said it in a sultry voice that was practically a purr.

Tom's eyes darted sideways to Lacey as if in terror. He took the hand Naomi had presented to him. "That's right," he said, with an air of uncertainty. "It's nice to meet you."

Naomi caressed Tom's hand under the guise of shaking it. "You never told me he was so handsome," she said as an aside to Lacey.

"I never got the chance," Lacey replied. "You were too busy freaking out about him being a serial killing cult leader."

Tom let out a nervous chuckle, his gaze darting between the sisters.

"Don't be silly!" Naomi exclaimed. "I said nothing of the sort."

Lacey rolled her eyes.

Tom attempted to free his hand from Naomi's clutches. "Lacey didn't tell me you were visiting," he said to her.

"Lacey didn't know," Naomi explained. "We wanted to surprise her."

"You did that, all right," Lacey commented wryly. Then, realizing poor Tom still wasn't free, she said sternly to her sister, "You can let go of him now."

As soon as Tom was finally released from Naomi, Shirley began stalking toward him. It was like watching wolves circling a baby deer, Lacey thought, deriving a small amount of amusement from the mental image.

Tom must have noticed Shirley's approach then, because his eyes widened. Her eyes were fixed on him with a look of curious judgment. Her arms were still wrapped around her flower-print bag like it was some kind of protective shield.

"This is my mom, Shirley," Lacey said wearily, gesturing to her. Her patience was running thin.

Tom looked as stunned as Lacey had a few minutes earlier. While she might not be ready for him to meet her mom, it looked like he wasn't ready for it either.

"It's wonderful to meet you," he said, in a polite, shell-shocked way.

He stepped forward as if to kiss her hello but the hold-on in her arms prevented him from getting close enough, so he stepped back again, then offered his hand instead. Shirley attempted to readjust her bag so she could free up a hand, but failed, so Tom let his hand fall and just stood there with a coy, uncertain smile on his lips.

Lacey couldn't help but find the whole exchange amusing. At least he was getting a taste of his own medicine! Maybe now he'd understand why she'd felt so awkward about being introduced to *his* mother, Heidi, while sitting in a police station as a murder suspect!

Shirley smiled. "It's a pleasure to meet you too," she said, though Lacey was quite certain her mom was sizing Tom up against her ex, David, whom Shirley still adored and still went to brunch with.

Just then, Frankie appeared from behind his grandmother. "I'm Frankie."

"Where did you come from?" Tom exclaimed jokingly. He peered around him in an exaggerated, theatrical manner. "Is that everyone? No one else is about to pop out of the woodwork, are they?"

Frankie giggled.

"Your accent is to die for!" Naomi exclaimed gleefully. "You're like the hero from a British rom-com."

Tom blushed under her smoldering gaze. "How long are you guys in town for?" he asked, his awkwardness doing little to dispel the image of him as the bumbling Brit Naomi was referring to. "Would you like to have dinner with us tonight?"

Horrified, Lacey snapped her gaze to meet his. "But you're supposed to be cooking me that special pie!"

"It's easy enough to size it up for five," Tom said, completely misunderstanding Lacey's comment. He looked at her family. "Would you guys like to try a traditional English pie?"

"Oh yes, you're a chef, aren't you?" Naomi purred. "Well, I for one would love to sample your goods . . ."

Lacey covered her eyes, cringing with embarrassment.

"That sounds wonderful," Shirley said. Evidently the offer of a home-cooked meal was all it took for her veil of suspicion to lift.

"Great!" Tom said, oblivious to Lacey's reticence. He pecked her on the cheek. "See you at seven. Enjoy your day, ladies!" He gave Frankie a friendly little fist bump. "And gent."

He headed out of the store and scurried across the road back to the safety of his patisserie. Lacey watched him go, feeling a heavy sensation in her chest that he'd haplessly just invited her family along on their well overdue date.

She turned back to her family, feeling anxious that the Tom-shaped buffer zone had now gone. It wasn't that she had a bad relationship with any of them, per se, there was just a lot of unspoken things between them, especially with regards to her father. After Francis (known affectionately as Frank back in the day) had left the family suddenly when Lacey was still a child, Shirley had refused to speak about him ever again. And even though Naomi named her only son after him, he was still never mentioned. In fact, it was never even acknowledged aloud that she'd done so. Shirley had immediately started calling him Frankie—probably to head off anyone else giving him Frank as a nick-name—and Naomi just pretended that she liked the name and there was nothing more to it. And since things left unspoken had a tendency to grow bigger and bigger and bigger—like black holes swallowing up everything and leaving behind nothing but antimatter—the mother-daughter-sister bond had been significantly impaired.

"So Lacey?" Shirley said with an expectant tone. "When are you going to show us around town?"

Frankie looked excited. "Yeah! Tour! Tour! I want to see the mountains."

"Wilfordshire doesn't have any mountains," Lacey began to say, before she was interrupted by the simultaneous voices of Naomi—"I want to go to a pub and order a pint of bitters"—and Shirley—"This place looks like something out of a movie!"

"No tour!" Lacey exclaimed, bringing her hands into a STOP gesture. But she said it far too loudly and far too firmly. Everyone fell silent, looking at her with dejected expressions.

"I have a store to run," Lacey said quickly, trying to explain herself. "I can't just drop everything without notice."

"'Course you can," Gina said, stepping in. "You left this morning to take Chester to the vet, didn't you?"

"All the more reason not to leave you again now," Lacey said, floundering.

"Nonsense," Gina replied. "I can mind the store. You know I'm always happy to. I've made that perfectly clear. And let's face it, you're always having to run off because of some unforeseen reason. What's another to add to the list?"

Clearly, Gina thought she was being helpful. She didn't realize that Lacey didn't actually want to spend the entire day with her family without having mentally psyched herself up for it!

"What about the Lodge?" Lacey asked, grasping desperately for an excuse. "Aren't you spending the afternoon working on the garden? You don't want to let Suzy down."

Gina chuckled. "I've finished my gardening duties at the Lodge. I'm all yours again. Besides, the garden here is starting to look a bit unloved. There are unpicked tomatoes rotting right on the vine, since a certain someone can't work out when they're ripe enough to pick." She flashed Lacey a pointed look.

"Lacey!" Shirley scolded, as if *she*, an apartment-dwelling New Yorker, had any idea whatsoever when to pick a vine-ripened tomato!

"Does that mean you're free today?" Frankie asked, sounding excited, as he tugged on her shirt.

"Uh-huh," Lacey said, forcing away her frustration for his sake. "I guess I am…"

A sick dog. A sudden family intrusion. Things were not going as planned for Lacey. And now that her family was coming along on her date, she couldn't help but wonder just how much worse they were about to get.

CHAPTER FOUR

"Can we go in here?" came Naomi's excited cry from behind Lacey.

Gritting her teeth, Lacey made an about-turn to face her sister.

So far, the family had made it to the end of the high street without bumping into any locals, a feat that had been far from easy. Lacey had maneuvered Shirley away from Taryn's boutique, and Frankie away from Jane's toy store, but now Naomi had stopped outside the Coach House Inn and was grinning excitedly up at it.

"We agreed to go to the beach first," Lacey reminded her, feeling like a teacher on a field trip attempting to herd a bunch of unruly pupils toward their destination.

While the beach would be busy, it was mainly filled with tourists, and their chances of anonymously blending in were far higher. But if they entered the Coach House Inn, bumping into a local was a given. And if Brenda the big-mouthed barmaid saw Lacey with her loud American family, the gossip would spread through town like wildfire. Lacey knew far too well how American tourists were perceived in this town, and she'd worked hard to lose her label as an outsider.

"But I want to order a pint of bitters," Naomi said, pouting like a grumpy child.

"No one calls it that," Lacey told her, growing exasperated. "And it's way too early for alcohol. Besides, Frankie won't be allowed in. He's too young."

"Really?" Naomi said, sounding surprised. "I thought all European children drank wine with every meal."

"Wine?" Frankie exclaimed with excitement, tugging on Lacey's shirt. "Can I drink wine?"

Lacey shook her head. "It's French kids who drink wine. The UK is just as strict as we are about alcohol."

It was a bluff. The drinking age in England was eighteen, and kids were allowed in most pubs during the day as long as they were with adults. But Naomi didn't need to know that.

"I really want to go to the beach," Shirley said. "It's been so long since I was at the ocean."

"See!" Lacey said, pouncing on the lifeline. "Let's walk along the promenade. Then we can look at the ancient ruined castle."

"Is it a Scottish castle?" Frankie asked, swinging Lacey's hand as they began to walk again.

"It's not Scottish," Lacey told him. "We're in England. Scotland is very far from here. And what is this whole Scotland obsession about anyway? Where did it even come from?"

Naomi rolled her eyes and answered on his behalf. "One of his school friends had a Braveheart-themed birthday party. Frankie made the ginger hair connection and it all spiraled from there. When Mom asked Frankie what he wanted for his eighth birthday, he had two requests—bagpipe lessons, or a trip on the Jacobite steam train in the Highlands. Luckily for everyone's eardrums, Mom had a bunch of air miles to use up."

"Lucky..." Lacey murmured under her breath.

"Hmm?" Naomi asked.

"Nothing," Lacey said.

She had to get over it, she reminded herself. Having her family here *was* nice. Getting to see Frankie was especially. She'd missed him over the last few months, and he'd grown a lot. He even seemed to have calmed down a little bit. It was just the shock of seeing them all without warning. And the timing. Such bad timing!

Lacey thought about her getaway with Tom. She was going to have to break it to her family sooner or later that she'd be leaving them to their own devices. But not right now. They'd only just set foot on British soil.

"Hey, Mom, look at this," Naomi called to Shirley. She'd paused outside an estate agent's and was gazing through the windows at the advertisements for sprawling farmhouse properties neither could afford but liked to imagine living in.

Lacey exhaled through her nostrils; they'd be stuck here forever now.

Just then, a female voice called from behind. "Lacey!"

Uh oh,' Lacey thought as she spun around to look back the way they'd come. Carol, the owner of Wilfordshire's famous bubble-gum-pink B&B, was hurrying along the cobblestones. Of all the people Lacey didn't want to bump into, Carol was rather high up on the list, just a couple of places behind her nemesis Taryn and Brenda the Big-Mouthed Barmaid. Lacey braced herself.

Carol reached her, her cheeks red from the effort of hurrying to catch up. Her gaze went straight to Frankie, who was clutching Lacey's hand.

"You've swapped your dog for a small boy?" Carol said, with a chuckle.

"Chester had to go to the vet," Lacey explained. "This is my nephew, Frankie. He's visiting me for a bit."

"Nephew?" Carol said. "I didn't even know you had one."

That's because you've never really taken the time to get to know me, Lacey thought, but did not say. "Well, I do," came her more diplomatic response.

"Let me give you one of these," Carol said, having already lost interest in the topic. She handed Lacey a bright pink flyer.

Lacey scanned the text and saw it was advertising a new discount at her B&B for the summer holidays. In black block writing, it proclaimed: *Cheaper than The Lodge, and a better breakfast too!*

Lacey thought of her friend Suzy, who had recently opened a rival B&B in the surrounding hillsides. Suzy had employed Lacey as the interior designer, and though the job hadn't quite gone to plan after the mayor was shot with an antique hunting rifle in the drawing room, the Lodge had successfully bounced back and was fast becoming the go-to B&B in Wilfordshire.

"I'm not sure it's legal to claim your breakfast is better than your competitor," Lacey told Carol, unimpressed.

"Piffle," Carol replied, batting the critique away with a flap of the hand. "Who's going to report me? I'm sure Superintendent Turner and DCI Lewis have far more important things to do than worry about the wording of a flyer!"

Lacey shuddered at the thought of Superintendent Karl Turner. She'd seen more of the arrogant cop than she cared to. Though his partner, Detective Chief Inspector Beth Lewis, was at least personable, Lacey still hoped she'd have no reason to see either ever again.

Just then, Shirley and Naomi appeared at her side, having grown bored of ogling through the estate agent's windows at the expensive country mansions far quicker than Lacey had anticipated.

"Carol," Lacey said, feeling her shoulders begin to tense, "this is my mom, Shirley, and my sister, Naomi. They flew over from New York this morning."

"Oh, how jolly wonderful to meet you," Carol trilled.

Naomi laughed. "It's jolly nice to meet you too," she said, attempting to speak in an English accent and failing miserably.

Carol stared at her. Lacey couldn't quite read her expression, but she didn't really need to, because in all likelihood, she was offended. Carol took any and every opportunity to be offended.

Lacey needed to salvage the conversation and quick, or Carol would be off gossiping about her rude family to all and sundry.

"Hey!" she exclaimed, hitting on a sudden brainwave. She waved the lurid pink flyer at her family. "Why don't I book you guys into Carol's B&B? As a treat on me. It's full of amazing decorations like pink flamingos," she said to Frankie, trying to appeal to his zany side. "And they serve the best English fry-up in Wilfordshire," she added, directing that to her foodie mother. "And since there's this extremely generous deal on at the moment," Lacey added, looking from Carol, who had puffed up with pride, to Naomi, her spendthrift of a sister, "I don't mind paying for it. What do you say? Treat on me?"

Lacey bit down on her lip, waiting expectantly for their response. Having them at the B&B would kill two birds with one stone for Lacey; they'd be out from under her nose (and she from under their scrutiny), and it would make it easier for her to escape to Dover when the time came. She hoped she'd put them in enough of a socially awkward situation that they'd feel unable to turn down the offer because it would risk offending Carol right to her face.

But, of course, that's not what happened. Lacey should've guessed as much.

Shirley took one look at the bright pink flyer and crinkled her nose with evident distaste. "That would be far too much to ask of you, Lacey," she said.

"Yeah, I want a sleepover at your house!" Frankie added. "I bet your cottage is full of cool decorations too."

"I agree with these two," Naomi said. "I'd prefer to stay at yours than at some strange B&B." She looked up at Carol and flippantly added, "No offense."

Carol, of course, took offense. In fact, she looked like she'd sucked on a particularly sour lemon. "Well," she said in a clipped tone, "I'll leave you to your family, Lacey. Put my flyer up in your store's window *if* you can be bothered. Or you can just throw it away like a piece of rubbish if you're so inclined."

And with that, she marched away, shoving pink flyers angrily at any unfortunate passerby who crossed her path.

Lacey deflated. Great. She'd been hoping that once she booked her family into the B&B and got them settled there, she'd be able to break the news of her and Tom's getaway more easily. But now she'd have to host them—and endure their criticisms of the home she loved but instinctively knew they would not—before unsettling them again when it came time for her and Tom to leave. She had to tell them about the getaway, and sooner rather than later.

Tonight, she decided. The homecooked pie would help soften the blow. Hopefully.

With a swirling apprehension in her stomach, Lacey knew her fun dinner date with Tom was going to be a far cry from the one she'd envisaged.

CHAPTER FIVE

"Tada!" Tom announced, as he came around the corner of the patisserie's kitchen carrying a ceramic dish in his oven-mittened hands.

Everyone clapped.

After their day trip to the beach, the family had returned to the patisserie, which Tom reserved just for them, like it was some kind of clandestine speakeasy's after-hours lock-in. Tom had even gone so far as to put out candles. A bottle of bubbly cooled in an ice bucket. It would've been so romantic, Lacey thought, if she hadn't been sharing the evening with her gate-crashing family.

Steam coiled from the dish as Tom set it on the table.

"What did you say this was called?" Shirley asked, rubbing her palms with relish.

"Homity pie." He began slicing it with a knife. "Or Devon pie, as we call it in my hometown. Although, come to think of it, I don't know if it was actually invented in Devon or whether we're just claiming it as our own."

He chuckled and placed a slice on a plate, handing it to Naomi.

"Looks like a quiche to me," Naomi said, taking the plate and holding it at eye-level like some kind of Health & Safety inspector.

Lacey kicked her under the table. "It's traditional British," she said through her teeth.

Tom didn't seem to take offense. He just smiled. "The recipes are very similar, it's true. Although there's potato in this, of course. We Brits love our potatoes."

"Yes, I've noticed that," Shirley said, prodding her slice skeptically with a fork. "Pie and mash. Fish and chips. Tell me, do you eat any other vegetables in England?"

26

Lacey rubbed her forehead with mounting irritation. Her mom was trying to show interest, but it sounded like the veiled criticism of a dispassionate food critic.

"Of course, Mom," she said, pointedly. "And I'm sure Tom doesn't want to sit here and list every one of them to you."

Shirley's brow furrowed, but Tom seemed not to have picked up on any of the undercurrents. He poured them each a glass of prosecco (and a fizzy apple juice for Frankie to make sure he was included), then took his seat.

"To family!" he said.

"Family!"

Family, Lacey thought, with a weary, internal sigh.

Everyone cheered, clinked their glasses, then tucked hungrily into their meals.

Despite the tenseness, Lacey's worries immediately melted away at the taste of Tom's signature buttery pastry. There was a hint of nutmeg mixed in with the onion and cheese filling, and Tom had even managed to sneak in some spinach without it overpowering the taste with its soggy, gritty bitterness.

"It's a miracle," Naomi commented. "Frankie's eating his greens."

"They're tasty," Frankie said, simply. "Not like how you make them, Mom."

Naomi pouted.

"The trick is to use good quality butter," Tom told her. "And to squeeze out any excess water."

"Where did you learn to cook?" Shirley asked, rather abruptly. She made it sound more like an interrogation than a question.

"I trained all over the globe," Tom said.

"Where?" Naomi asked. It was her turn to interrupt.

Tom looked right again. "Italy. India. The Netherlands. Portugal. I spent a year in Paris perfecting the croissant."

"What about Scotland?" Frankie asked, getting in on the table-tennis match poor Tom was caught in.

"Frankie," Naomi warned.

"What?" Frankie protested.

Tom just smiled, seemingly unfazed. "I've been to Scotland," he told Frankie.

The young boy's eyes lit up. "Did you learn how to make haggis?"

27

"I did."

"Wow . . ." Frankie said, breathless with wonder.

"And . . ." Tom added, "I also learned how to make tatties and neeps, and I got the best recipe for cullen skink."

Frankie started laughing.

It warmed Lacey's heart to see how calm and patient Tom was with her nephew. Frankie seemed to have taken a real shine to Tom. He didn't have any male role models in his life—a missing grandfather, no idea who his biological dad was, and now not even David as an uncle—so it wasn't exactly surprising he was drawn to him. But it was a relief that at least one person in her family was behaving cordially, especially considering Naomi was acting like a googly-eyed teenager and Shirley was still taking some time to thaw.

"You're quite accomplished, aren't you?" came Shirley's frosty voice. Her eyes were fixed on her prosecco as she swirled it round and round in her glass.

Her tone wasn't lost on Lacey. Her mom was obviously comparing Tom's cooking achievements to David's business ones, which wasn't a fair comparison in Lacey's opinion. David and Tom were like chalk and cheese. Besides, following your father into the family business wasn't the same as striking out on your own, starting your own business, and pursuing your life's passion, as far as Lacey was concerned.

"Thank you," Tom said, forever and always unable to pick up on the unspoken undercurrents of conversation. It was a habit that annoyed Lacey in terms of all things romantic, but was actually rather handy in this scenario.

"Can we let the poor chef eat some food?" Lacey said with exasperation. She gestured to Tom's pie, which he'd not yet even taken a bite of. "All these questions are making me dizzy."

Lacey very much wanted to talk to Tom alone about their upcoming getaway and how to break the news to her family. But she didn't get the chance. Because of course her family didn't actually listen to her when she asked them to stop grilling Tom, and the conversation went right back to a rapid-fire round with Tom in the hot seat.

Still, she was actually kind of enjoying herself. Or at least, successfully tolerating her family's presence. And watching Frankie's puppy dog expression for Tom was rather sweet.

She decided not to ruin the moment with the news. She buttoned her lips. Though she'd have to bite the bullet sooner or later, for now, she was choosing later.

It was dark by the time the taxi took them from the patisserie to the drive of Crag Cottage. Its headlamps illuminated the front of the old stone cottage, and despite the copious amounts of prosecco swirling in her stomach, Lacey felt a sudden pang of anxiety about what her family would think of her home. It was a far cry from her and David's swanky apartment in New York City, which had been modern and sleek. But it meant so much to her. It was hers, and hers alone. There was a whole lot of pride bound up in those jagged stone bricks.

Naomi perched on the edge of the taxi's black pleather seat, craning her neck to peer through the windshield. "You live *here?*" she asked, using that tone of disbelief she'd used so frequently over the years it had long lost its intended effect. ("You're marrying *him?*" "You're wearing *that?*" "You're moving *there?*")

"Yup," Lacey replied, mustering her confidence like a shield.

Naomi unfurled her long legs from the back seat of the taxi and strode off across the lawn.

Lacey kept her eyes on her sister as she handed a ten-pound note through the partition to the driver up front. Naomi was heading for the cliff, and the combination of soft grass, high heels, darkness, and a prosecco-laced bloodstream set Lacey's nerves on edge. She quickly followed her sister, leaving her mom to deal with a snoring Frankie and a trunk full of luggage.

"Hey, sis, watch where you're going!" Lacey called, hurrying across the moonlit grass after her.

"You live by the ocean?" Naomi called over her shoulder.

This time, her "tone" was absent, Lacey noted. She was being genuine.

"Nice, huh?" Lacey said, drawing up to her side.

Naomi stayed silent. Her gaze was fixed outward at the churning, dark sea. The breeze stirred through her hair. She tightened her arms around her middle.

"It's just like when we were kids," she finally said. "When we came on vacation here with Dad."

Lacey studied her profile. Naomi *never* talked about the past if she could avoid it. "You remember that?" she asked.

"Of course," came her sister's wistful reply. She glanced over at Lacey, the white moon reflecting in her dark pupils. "There are some things you never forget."

"Girls?" came Shirley's sudden shrill exclamation.

Lacey tore her gaze from Naomi and over to the cottage porch. Shirley was standing there, surrounded by suitcases and bags, with a half-asleep Frankie propped up against the door.

"Will you stop jabbering and help?" Shirley continued. "It's freezing!"

It was far from freezing on the warm summer evening, but Lacey hurried toward her anyway. As the elder sister, obedience had been drummed into her in a way it had not been with Naomi. She left the cryptic comment hanging in the air beside the cliffs.

Crag Cottage felt extra small with her family inside, even though Lacey had hosted larger parties before. They were just such big presences to her. It seemed as if the low ceilings were sinking, the narrow walls encroaching...

She led them straight into the kitchen. Of all the rooms in the cottage, the English-country rustic kitchen was her pride and joy. From the array of bronze pots hanging from hooks, to the genuine Aga and white porcelain farmer's sink, everything in this room was precious to her.

"This is nice," Naomi said, dispassionately.

"Say it once more with feeling," Lacey joked wryly.

"I mean it!" Naomi contested. "It's very...rustic."

"It's like a farmer's house," Frankie said through a sleepy yawn.

"A stylish farmer's house," Naomi added, hurriedly.

"I mean the smell," Frankie said. "The doggie smell. And...is that manure?"

Naomi forced out a laugh over his comments. "Frankie's so sleepy he's practically delirious!" she said loudly.

But Lacey didn't mind because she knew Frankie's comments weren't intended to be malicious. The smell of her neighbor's sheep was rather pungent at times, especially now the weather was warming up and the lambs were getting bigger. Besides, Frankie was just a little kid. It was her mom's and sister's opinions that really mattered to her.

"It's exactly what I was expecting it to be," Shirley said.

"What's that supposed to mean?" Lacey asked. But she knew what her mom was implying. Lacey had inherited her father's taste—antiques, cottages by the ocean, quaint British towns—and Shirley was more than acutely aware of it. It still stung Lacey to know there was a whole side to her that her mother would never, ever approve of.

"I just mean that whole Upper East Side apartment thing was never really you," Shirley said, back-tracking. "That's more Naomi's type of thing. I always pictured you by a cottage overlooking the ocean."

If Shirley was attempting to dig herself out of a hole she was only making it worse.

"I suppose we should figure out the sleeping arrangements," Lacey said stiffly. "I'm not sure where I'm going to fit you all. I only have one guest room."

"I can take the guest room," Shirley said, as if she was making a generous sacrifice.

Lacey looked at Naomi. "Do you and Frankie want to share the master bedroom? There's a double bed in there. Or is Frankie too old?"

Naomi ruffled her sleeping son's auburn curls. "I think Frankie's too tired to care for one night. But we might have to build him a fort in the corner for the rest of the time though."

She laughed, and Lacey tensed as she remembered the upcoming trip she'd not yet told her family about. Though Naomi had actually provided her with an opening, now felt far from the opportune moment to bring it up. Not while Shirley was doing her disapproving chin-tip, and while Frankie was swaying with exhaustion, and Naomi was . . . well, it was never a good time to give Naomi bad news.

So Lacey took the coward's way out and retreated to the living room to sleep on the sofa.

As she lay in the living room, staring up at the ceiling, she felt Chester's absence more than ever. She could just picture him in the vet's holding kennel, looking forlorn and lonely. The poor thing was probably so confused, unable to comprehend what was happening to him. And he'd have two whole weeks to endure it! At least *her* discomfort would only last a few nights.

Thinking of Chester made Lacey come to a personal resolution. It was time to stop beating about the bush. Tomorrow, she'd tell her family that she and Tom had a pre-booked trip away and that she'd be leaving them here in

Wilfordshire to fend for themselves. Perhaps then they'd learn that next time they felt like visiting, they should check with her first.

Pigs might fly . . . came Lacey's final thought before she drifted off to sleep.

Lacey stirred awake on the sofa. Every single one of her muscles was stiff and achy. The sofa was droopy at the best of times. After eight hours under the weight of a slumbering person, it had practically disintegrated.

Lacey stretched, groaning as her body protested.

Daylight was coming through a gap in the cream-colored curtains. But the house was quiet. Unusually quiet.

"Chester," Lacey said, sadly, remembering her pooch a couple miles away, locked in a kennel at the vet's.

Her English Shepherd was as reliable as an alarm clock, nudging her awake at seven a.m. sharp so he could complete his morning jog around the lawns, dispersing any sheep who'd accidentally strayed over the boundaries of Gina's garden during the night, before chowing down a quick bowl of kibble while Lacey downed an espresso, searching his hiding spots for where he'd left his favorite tennis ball, then sitting on the kitchen mat barking up at his leash because he was now ready for his walk along the beach to the store, thank you very much.

But the silence seemed even more pronounced than just the fact that Chester wasn't there. It sounded suspiciously like *no one* was. And since her family wasn't exactly known for their conspicuousness, Lacey realized that could only mean one thing. They'd left!

She jumped off the couch, discarding the throw she'd been using as a blanket, and hurried out of the room on bare feet. She went straight for the kitchen. Two crumb-covered plates sat on the table, beside an empty cereal bowl with just a residue of milk left behind and a couple of corn flakes floating soggily at the bottom. Two mugs of drained coffee, one of juice. Dirtied knives and forks. No jackets hanging up on the hooks by the kitchen door. No shoes on the mat.

"They've gone!" Lacey exclaimed.

The thought of her family out there in her town without supervision sent a bolt of dread through Lacey. They could meet *anyone*. Say *anything*! She had to find them!

She peeled through the house, gathering her things for the day, before heading outside.

Where did you guys go? she texted frantically to Naomi as she hurried up the garden path and onto the lane.

We went to town for breakfast, came Naomi's reply.

Where? Lacey typed back, thinking of the coffee shop on the corner owned by the woman who had accused her of murder, or the cafe a little farther up that had been hostile toward an American opening up shop in the high street. There were so many places Lacey didn't want them to be!

No message was forthcoming from Naomi. Lacey pressed onward.

Reaching the bottom of the high street, Lacey began crisscrossing the cobblestones from one side to the next, checking in through each window as she ran. They weren't in the coffee shop (thankfully), nor the cafe. They also weren't in the baker's, or any of the cute tea rooms with their pastel-colored brickwork and gingham curtains, the quaintness of which would usually be an irresistible lure to a sentimental foodie like her mom.

"Where are they?" Lacey muttered aloud.

She'd almost gotten as far as her antiques store when she suddenly caught sight of a flash of orange. She turned her head and saw the distinct ginger girls of Frankie through the window of Tom's patisserie.

"Oh no . . ." Lacey murmured aloud, hastening her step.

Her view through the window grew sharper as she approached. Sitting beside Frankie were her mom and Naomi. Then there was Tom. They were all grinning widely, as if sharing a moment of excitement and delight.

Her stomach churned as she shoved open the door and burst inside.

Everyone turned at the sound of the aggressively jangling bell.

"Lacey," Tom said, beaming. "Great news. Your family is coming to Dover with us!"

CHAPTER SIX

L acey grasped Tom by the elbow and steered him into the patisserie's kitchen. "What are you doing?" she hissed.

"What do you mean?" he asked, sounding bemused.

"You invited my family on our romantic getaway to Dover?"

Tom shrugged. "They flew all the way over from New York," he said simply. "We can't just head off on our trip and leave them here. It would be rude, for one." He took a step forward and touched her upper arms affectionately. "And anyway, it'll be a good opportunity for me to get to know them better. Which means getting to know *you* better. It's not like you're going to tell me all your embarrassing childhood anecdotes, are you?"

He gave her a tender smile, but it did nothing to mollify Lacey. She put her hands on her hips.

"But where will they fit? I'm not going to sleep on a sofa again!"

Tom gave her arms a reassuring squeeze. "Relax. This was going to be a surprise, but the inn is actually a recently converted lighthouse. I booked the main suite but there's an option to rent out the whole thing. I'll call the owner up and book the other rooms, okay? There'll be more than enough space for all of us."

A lighthouse? Goodness! If Tom hadn't sprung it on her in such stressful circumstances, Lacey would have been thrilled. It sounded so unique! So exotic! But instead, her mind was too clouded by shock to feel anything but frustration.

"You really should've asked me first," she mumbled.

Tom regarded her with a perplexed expression. "I thought you'd want to spend time with your family. I didn't realize it would upset you."

"I'm not upset," Lacey countered immediately, though the complexity and nuance of how she was feeling was too difficult for her to process, let alone explain. "I just wanted to spend time with *you*," she said, exhaling.

"Good news," Tom said, with a mischievous grin. "I'm coming too."

But his quip failed to cheer Lacey. It was just so typical of Tom. They were supposed to be having a *romantic* getaway—indeed, their *first* romantic getaway! But with her family tagging along, any chance of candlelit dinners or champagne and strawberries or naked Jacuzzis would be well and truly out of the question. Yet Tom just didn't seem to care about that at all.

Lacey couldn't find the words to express what she was thinking. So she just gave him a sad smile and finally said, "Yes. I suppose you are."

"You don't think I'm being selfish, do you?" Lacey said, letting out a deep sigh. "It's just I was really excited about having some time for just me and Tom and then he invited them along. I mean, can you actually believe it?"

She stared into Chester's knowing dark brown eyes. He whinnied his acknowledgment and she petted his velvety ears.

"Thanks," Lacey murmured. "I knew you'd understand."

Just then, Lakshmi appeared at the door in her dark green scrubs. She looked down at Lacey and Chester snuggled together on the floor beside the open kennel. "Are you all right down there?"

Lacey nodded. She'd come straight from Tom's to the vet's to get some much needed sympathy from Chester, who she knew wouldn't judge her in the same way Gina likely would. She also wanted to say goodbye, because this would be the last time she'd see him now for a few days.

"I just needed a therapy session," Lacey joked. She wriggled her legs out from beneath Chester, where he'd draped himself across her. "Gina's coming to see you tomorrow," she told him.

Chester looked at her sadly.

"Oh boy, don't give me that face," Lacey said. "You love Gina."

Chester huffed through his nostrils, then dutifully trotted into his kennel with his tail hanging dejectedly down. Lacey felt a pang of guilt.

"Is he okay in there?" she asked Lakshmi, filled with worry.

Lakshmi closed the kennel door and bolted it. Chester peered forlornly through the glass.

"He's fine," Lakshmi assured her. "He's responding well to his pills. Did you say someone else will be visiting him while you're in Dover?"

Lacey felt her cheeks start to go warm. Lakshmi must've overheard her whole conversation with Chester, right down to her complaining about Tom inviting her family to Dover.

She scratched her neck awkwardly. "You heard all that, huh?"

Lakshmi chuckled. "Uh-huh. 'Fraid so. But don't worry, I don't think you're being selfish at all." She lowered her voice. "I go on vacations to get *away* from my mother. If someone invited her along, I'd be livid."

Lacey chuckled too. "I'm glad I'm not the only one."

With her spirits slightly lifted, she left Chester in the capable care of Lakshmi and headed back to her store.

Her mom, sister, and nephew were all inside when she entered. Frankie was sat on the floor playing with Boudica while Naomi sat in the window seat flicking through a gossip magazine. Shirley was sitting straight-backed on the red velvet loveseat, her expression a mixture of discomfort and boredom.

"There she is!" Gina exclaimed as the brass doorbell softly tinkled in Lacey's entry.

"Lacey," Shirley said, using the same tone she used to when Lacey had done something naughty as a child. "Where on earth did you disappear to?"

"Sorry," Lacey mumbled. "I had to go and say goodbye to Chester at the vet's. I thought I said so."

She knew full well she hadn't, that she'd just left Tom's in a complete daze, but a little white lie was sometimes necessary to prevent a bigger argument.

"Gina's been telling me all about Punch and Judy," Frankie piped up. "I want to buy the clown but Mom said I can't."

"He creeps me out," Naomi said, grimacing at the marionette. "And you only want him because he has ginger hair. You'll never play with him."

Lacey shot Gina an apologetic look. It hadn't occurred to her that her friend would be lumped with her family while she was busy having a therapy session with Chester. But far from looking stressed, Gina actually seemed rather buoyant. She was a people person, after all, Lacey reasoned. And she didn't have the same *history* Lacey did with them either.

"So what are we going to do today?" Shirley asked, in her slightly clipped manner. "I don't want to sit around in your store forever." Though she didn't say it aloud, it was obvious Shirley was less than comfortable in Lacey's antiques store. Her crinkled nose and guarded posture were a dead giveaway.

Naomi joined in. "Yeah, Lacey, what are we going to do today? We've seen the beach. The cliffs. The sheep. We've had freshly baked pastries and tea from a pot. What else is there to do around here?"

"Tom said we should have cream tea in the afternoon," Frankie said. He looked at Lacey quizzically. "What's cream tea? Is it kinda like a hot milkshake?"

Lacey chuckled. "I can see how you'd come to that conclusion, but no, cream tea isn't a hot milkshake. Cream tea is where you have a scone with jam and clotted cream and a cup of tea," she told him.

"Scones!" Frankie repeated. "I've had them. Mom makes them for me on special occasions."

Surprised, Lacey looked over at her sister. Naomi was pretending not to be listening to the conversation anymore, for the very obvious reason that the person who introduced them to scones in the first place had been their father, and he'd done so in Wilfordshire no less.

"Well, Wilfordshire has the best scones in the whole of the UK," Lacey said, turning back to Frankie. "You have to try them before you go. I can recommend a lovely tearoom out in the hillsides, and there's a stately home there too called Penrose Manor." If her family went all the way out to the estate, she'd get at least a couple of hours' respite from them before the getaway forced them into even closer quarters.

"More food?" Shirley said with a disdainful sigh. "Honestly, why aren't all the English overweight? There seems to be a meal between every meal."

Gina started to laugh. She patted her slightly rotund belly. "Some of us are."

Boudica let out a small noise as if in protest of her owner's self-deprecation.

"Can't we stay here?" Frankie asked. He was sitting cross-legged on the floor beside an open trunk, surrounded by antique toys.

"You'll get bored of that in five minutes," Naomi commented.

Shirley looked displeased at Frankie's request. "No, Frankie. Grandma doesn't want to sit around in a dark, dusty room all day. It's bad for my lungs. And I can't say I like the smell very much."

Don't like the memories, more like, Lacey thought, her mind going to her father's old antiques store in New York City. But of course, Lacey didn't say anything aloud. Mentioning her father was a sin.

Frankie stood, leaving his pile of toys on the floor, and headed for the door. Naomi and Shirley followed after him.

"At least we only have one day to kill here," Naomi said to Shirley as she opened the door. "We'll be off to Dover tomorrow."

The bell jangled as they closed the door behind them.

As soon as they were gone, Lacey flopped forward and let out a deep sigh. She highly doubted there would be anything in the quaint seaside town of Dover to keep her family occupied if Wilfordshire had bored them so quickly.

Gina started to chuckle. "Call me mad, but I could've sworn your sister just said they were going to Dover tomorrow."

Lacey raised her weary eyes at her friend and nodded sadly. "Tom invited them along."

Behind her red-framed spectacles, Gina's eyes widened. "Oh."

"Oh indeed," Lacey replied, sinking her head into her hands.

It was going to be a very long trip.

CHAPTER SEVEN

"This is your car?" Naomi said, bright and early the next morning. She used her "tone" as she heaved her case into the trunk of the Volvo. "I mean, you traded up in terms of men, but what the heck happened to your taste in vehicles?"

"I needed something to get around," Lacey replied, feeling defensive of her uniquely ugly secondhand sedan. "I didn't realize I was going to settle down here in Wilfordshire." She dumped her bags in the trunk of the car. "Besides, I've grown to love it."

Naomi rolled her eyes. "You made your life here sound so boho, Lacey. Turns out, it was actually hobo."

She chuckled at her own scathing joke, then got into the back of the car. Lacey took a deep breath to calm her already fraying nerves.

She'd managed to make it through another night with her family, mainly thanks to Tom's calming presence and suggestion they watch a three-hour epic fantasy movie. It even seemed as if Shirley was starting to warm up to him a little, and it had only taken two more restaurant-quality homecooked meals in addition to the homity pie to get her there. Tom's prawn linguine had gone down a storm, and his surprise hot cross buns for breakfast seemed to have sealed the deal.

Just then, Tom appeared at her side, his arms laden with luggage. The floral print one was a dead giveaway for Shirley's.

"Did my mom make you carry her bags?" Lacey asked, taking one off him. "Like some kind of footman?" She was mortified.

"I offered," Tom said, like it was no big deal.

Frankie skipped out through the door of Crag Cottage and up to the car, beelining for the front passenger seat door. He yelled "Shotgun!" and dive bombed inside.

"I don't think so, mister," Lacey said, marching up to the passenger side before he got the chance to shut the door. "That's Tom's seat."

"But I get carsick," Frankie said.

Naomi poked her head out from the back seat and added, "He does. Better let him sit up front, sis. We don't want him puking."

Lacey ground her teeth.

Tom gave her a sympathetic look as he handed her a piece of paper.

"What's this?" she asked.

"Directions to the inn," he said, before slipping into the back seat.

Lacey unfolded the paper and saw she was looking at much, much more than just plain old directions. Tom had used the same artistic talents he used to construct his macaron statues for the patisserie's display window to hand draw, in ink, a map of the town they were going to in Dover. It was called Studdleton Bay, and by the way he'd captured it, it looked absolutely delightful. The small town had many different labels on it, indicating museums, churches, and fancy restaurants he wanted them to visit during their trip. There was a beach for sunbathing, cliffs for walking, and even the lighthouse inn they were staying at had been drawn, with little ink versions of the two of them waving from its windows. Just like the photographs, the map was another piece of the romantic getaway Tom had planned, to make it extra special.

She looked over at him in the backseat beside Naomi and Shirley, squeezed thigh to thigh with the two of them.

Just where they wanted him, Lacey thought glumly, as she folded the directions back up and slid them into her pocket.

"Auntie Lacey!" Frankie screeched from the passenger seat. "Can we listen to bagpipe music?"

Lacey took a deep, steadying breath. This was going to be a very trying few hours.

"Frankie, for the hundredth time, we're not going to Scotland," Lacey said.

Her head was pounding from an hour's worth of facts about Loch Ness and the Highlands and how to make haggis. Frankie's incessant enthusiasm for all things Scottish had also had the secondary effect of excluding her from the backseat chatter of Tom, Shirley, and Naomi. The three of them seemed to be getting on like a house on fire, laughing away at some inside joke they already had. Lacey knew she ought to be thankful her new lover and her family were getting on, but she was still annoyed about their intrusion on her romantic getaway.

"Did you know that there's over seven thousand different styles of tartan?" Frankie said.

Lacey exhaled slowly. "I did know that. Because you already told me. Several times."

"Look!" Naomi suddenly screeched from the backseat, loud enough to almost give Lacey a heart attack. "There's the sign for Studdleton Bay!"

Indeed, coming up on the left-hand side was a bright blue highway sign, with white writing proclaiming their distance to the small Dover town of Studdleton Bay. Beneath, it stated:

Deal . . . 8 miles

Sandwich Bay . . . 15 miles

"Sandwich Bay?" Lacey read aloud. "Is that what the sandwich picture was about?"

She finally put the final photographic clue Tom had sent her into place.

"You only just worked that out?" Tom said with a laugh. "What did you think the sandwich was for?"

"I just assumed there was a famous type of Dover sandwich I didn't know about," Lacey told him.

Her shoulders started to shake from chuckling. It felt nice to interact with Tom for what felt like the first time since they'd set off early this morning. But before she had a chance to continue the conversation, another name on the sign made her heart almost stop beating. *Canterbury.*

All at once, Lacey saw in her mind's eye the text message she'd received from Xavier Santino. When she'd tried to distance herself from him—concerned that he may have a secondary ulterior romantic motive for helping her—he'd sent a message saying he knew where her father was. Apparently there'd been a recent sighting of Francis in Canterbury, but Xavier had been so vague on the details and unable to provide any specifics, she'd just thought it was a desperate ploy to maintain contact with her. But now, seeing the word printed like that made it seem suddenly possible. Could her father be a mere twenty miles away from her getaway location?

But her thoughts were immediately distracted by Frankie.

"Look! Look!" he cried, pointing with excitement.

In the not too far distance, a silver streak of ocean had appeared on the horizon. It was such a sunny day, the water was glittering. Overhead, flocks of seagulls undulated over the waves. And there, the craggy cliffs of cream-colored, crumbly chalk appeared. The world famous White Cliffs of Dover.

Lacey felt a thrill run through her. She wasn't going to let anything bring her down. No matter how much her family got on her nerves, or how often thoughts of her father crowded her mind, she was going to enjoy this beautiful place, this wonderful summer, and these days without responsibility.

Just as long as they didn't murder each other first.

Chapter Eight

"Oh, Tom, it looks amazing," Lacey gushed, catching his eye in the rearview mirror.

He smiled in response, but didn't get a chance to say anything, because Frankie was pointing excitedly out the window, exclaiming, "There's a castle on that hill! A castle!"

"And look at that gorgeous church," Shirley added, gesturing to a tall, gray-stone building with a formidably high steeple.

Everyone continued to coo at the pretty Dover countryside as Lacey drove them through the lush green hillsides and into the cute chocolate box village of Studdleton Bay. Here, the architecture was a mixture of old stone cottages, three-story Edwardian townhouses, and large, grand, brick Georgian heritage buildings, with the occasional crumbling ruins of a Norman church thrown in for fun. Union Jack flags fluttered above the doorways, and hanging baskets filled with bright pink flowers decorated every lamp post.

After a couple more turns, the red-domed tip of a lighthouse appeared in the distance.

"That's not it…" Lacey said, excitement mounting in her chest.

"I think it is…" Tom replied, his grin audible.

"It can't be!" Lacey stammered in disbelief.

More and more of the red-and-white-striped lighthouse came into view and all Lacey could do was gaze at it in breathless wonder. It was such a unique idea of Tom's. So adventurous. So romantic. David had never brought her to places like this. He liked his hotels sleek, clean, and luxurious. He'd never rough it on the rugged cliffs of Dover in a decked-out lighthouse. Lacey's heart swelled with gratitude as she caught Tom's reflection in the rearview mirror. How had she gotten so lucky?

"It looks like a lollipop!" Frankie cried from the passenger seat beside her.

"It looks like it's from that fantasy movie we watched last night," Shirley added.

"It looks like ... it's on a farm?" Naomi said.

She was right. Just as Lacey took the final turning, the smell of animal droppings wafted through the cracked windows. A wooden sign hammered into the ground read *Ashworth's Farm*, and a cluster of chickens went scurrying in front of them.

"Watch out, Auntie Lacey!" Frankie cried.

"Don't worry, I saw them," Lacey said, slowing her Volvo to a crawl. It bumped along the uneven ground.

"Slow down, will you?" Shirley commanded from the back seat. "All this bumping is making me feel sick. And the smell!" She pinched her nose. She'd gone slightly green.

"I'm going five miles an hour, Mom," Lacey told her. "I can't go much slower."

So much for romantic, Lacey thought. Her family were going to whine about everything and spoil all her fun. At least she and Tom would get some privacy at night; the lighthouse looked enormous, as though ten people could easily occupy it.

As they crawled along the path toward the lighthouse inn, a large wooden cattle barn appeared to their left. A sign over the door said, *Reception and Tea Rooms*. Another sign directed them to the *car park*.

Lacey let out a giddy giggle.

"Car park," Frankie said, in a British accent. "Carrrr parrrrk."

Lacey passed the barn, and the farmyard site opened up. To her surprise, there were a number of tents pitched up in the grass, and several other cars parked in a higgledy-piggledy fashion in the lot, which was really just a patch of worn, muddy ground.

"There's camping here as well?" Lacey asked Tom, trying to keep the sound of reticence out of her voice.

"Yeah, but the inn's owner assured me we won't notice them. They have a no music at night policy."

"Okay," Lacey said, though she was still uncertain.

She parked and the family tumbled out, stretching their aching limbs.

"I guess we check in at the barn," Tom said.

They headed back along the path, passing the pitched tents where two toddlers in swimsuits were picking daisies in the sunshine while their parents watched on from fold-out chairs.

"It's so hot," Naomi said, fanning her face. "I had no idea England could be hot like this."

"We get a week or two of solid sun if we're lucky," Tom told her. "But I've had plenty of English summers in my time where it's rained every single day."

They reached the barn. Several elaborate wind chimes were hung outside, and they let out an inviting tinkle.

Inside, the barn was decorated in a hodgepodge of garden furniture. Pastel-colored bunting crisscrossed around the ceiling. Fresh farm foods were on sale, like goat cheese, milk, butter, and organic eggs.

On the left of the store was a counter made of beech wood, surrounded by shelving units displaying jars of edible delights—pickles, jams, honey, and relishes—and cookbooks. In the middle of all the clutter sat a calico cat in a wicker basket, taking great pains to lick its claw pads. Behind the counter stood a woman with mousy straight brown hair that hung to her shoulders. A purple velvet headband kept the stray hairs off her face.

She looked up from where she was arranging bright pink and yellow tulips in a vase. "Can I help?"

"I have a booking for Forrester," Tom said, stepping forward.

The woman smiled, and laughter lines appeared beside her eyes. "Ah. You're the guests for the lighthouse, aren't you?" She put down her tulips and pulled a pencil stub out from behind her ear. She quickly wrote something down in a book beside the till in neat, flowery writing. "You're all checked in. Follow me."

Lacey felt a thrill of anticipation ripple through her as the woman grabbed a set of keys from a hook, gave the calico a tickle behind the ears, then headed out from around the counter and gestured to the entrance of the barn.

Everyone followed.

As they strolled along the path toward the lighthouse, a bunch of chickens of all different colors started to follow them, their feathers shimmering in the sunlight. Lacey laughed, delighted by the sight. She never knew chickens could be so attractive!

The woman bent down and scooped up one of the chickens, cradling it in her arm as she walked. "I'm Helen, by the way," she said. "This is Trixie, the soppy chicken. She loves a cuddle. Rosie on the other hand..." She pointed at the white-feathered chicken leading the pack with an air of self-importance. "She's a mean one."

Frankie looked amazed by the whole spectacle. "Is there a rooster?"

"Oh yes," Helen said. "Leonard. He thinks he rules the harem, but really the women are in command. You'll hear him first thing at dawn."

"Awesome," Frankie whispered under his breath.

"Your farm is so beautiful," Lacey gushed.

"Thank you," Helen replied.

"Yes, it's a wonderful piece of real estate," Shirley added as she took a cautious step over a pile of what looked suspiciously like chicken droppings. "A lighthouse! How did you come to own that?"

"I've had the farm and barn for years," Helen began, "and it was always a dream of mine to run a B&B one day." As she spoke, she caressed the top of Trixie's head. The hen cooed like a dove, and burrowed lovingly into her neck. "The lighthouse used to be owned by an old man who just used it as storage, which was just such a waste in my opinion. Anyway, he passed away not that long ago and luckily for me, his family decided to sell. I snapped it up straight away, got stuck in with the DIY, and ta-da!" She gestured to the lighthouse's wooden door, which had so recently been painted a bright mailbox red, it still smelled fresh. "A B&B!"

"A true entrepreneur," Shirley said, sounding impressed. Lacey hoped some of Helen's spirit might rub off on how her mom perceived her own escape to the country and desire to start a new life.

"I like to think so," Helen said. She placed Trixie down at her feet. The chickens dispersed in a flurry of clucks and feathers. Helen retrieved a key from her pocket. "Better a B&B than a storage space, in my opinion." She wiggled the key in the lock. "The space is perfect for it, as well," she added, twisting the key back and forth; it was clearly a little rusty. "The space is very versatile, so I was able to divide it into separate suites. It means there's the option for flexibility for my guests. Some want the whole B&B experience with breakfast served in the barn, others prefer to self-cater."

"I told you," Tom said knowingly to Lacey. "Didn't I say there'd be plenty of privacy even with five of us?" He chuckled. Then, as an aside to Helen he added, "Lacey thought we'd all be sharing a room!"

The door finally swung open, but Helen didn't step over the threshold. In fact, she froze in place. Then she slowly turned and looked at them, her eyes scanning from Shirley to Naomi to Frankie, as if fully perceiving them for the first time. Frankie flashed her one of his characteristically cheeky grins.

"Is something the matter?" Tom asked.

Helen had gone quite pale. "I think . . . I made a mistake," she stammered. "A misunderstanding. When you called to say you needed more space because more people were coming, I thought you just needed extra *beds*."

"So we don't have the whole thing?" Lacey asked, a feeling of dread rising through her.

"No," Helen confirmed. "There's a couple renting the ground floor. You have the suite at the top with extra beds."

"What kind of beds?" Shirley asked.

Helen was slow to answer. Her voice was small. "Camp beds."

Naomi exhaled with frustration. "I'm not sleeping on a camp bed."

Lacey closed her eyes. Perfect. This was just perfect.

"So we are sharing a room," she said.

Helen looked mortified. "I'm so sorry . . . Just as soon as the couple on the ground floor check out, I'll open up the whole space." She pointed at the green wooden door to the left of the spiral staircase, which was firmly shut. "They're only here for the long weekend."

"We're only here for the long weekend," Lacey replied, her chest sinking.

"It's fine," Tom jumped in, using his happy-go-lucky, reassuring tone. "We don't mind! Frankie's okay with a camp bed, aren't you, chum?"

"You bet!" Frankie said.

Of course he is, Lacey thought. For a child of eight it was all part of the adventure. For a grown woman approaching forty, however, it was a completely different story!

"Shirley and Naomi can share the master bed if they don't want the camp beds," Tom continued, well and truly in what Gina referred to as his "Genial English Gentleman Problem Solver Mode."

"Yes, I suppose that's okay," Shirley said, looking somewhat put-out by the arrangement.

Tom looked over at Lacey. "And we'll take the camp beds. We don't mind roughing it a bit, do we, Lacey?"

Lacey gritted her teeth. Of course Tom didn't mind. He was a mountain-biking, tent-sleeping, fish-catching, outdoorsy type. And, unlike her, he hadn't spent the last two nights sleeping on a saggy couch!

But the thing that bothered Lacey the most was that Tom clearly had no concern about their lack of privacy at all. With how the sleeping arrangements had panned out, they wouldn't even be able to innocently cuddle one another! But Tom was acting like he didn't give two hoots about the complete lack of romance their so-called romantic getaway would involve.

"Lacey?" he prompted, when she remained silent. "We don't mind, do we?"

"Not at all," she finally said, with a sigh of resignation.

Far from the rom-com she was hoping for, this getaway was turning into a straight up tragedy.

Chapter Nine

Lacey tried to put the mix-up over the accommodations out of her mind as the family hauled their cases into the lighthouse and up the wooden spiral staircase. The place *was* amazing, after all. The lighthouse was decorated in a rustic beach-house style, with pale wooden floors and powder-blue furnishings. The kitchen was amply sized for Tom to cook in, and, by the sounds of his delighted exclamations as he sifted through all the pots and pans, it was well stocked with a range of good-quality items with which to do it.

Enormous windows circled the entirety of the floor, letting in so much light it was a bit like being in a greenhouse. There was also a great view over the town, which seemed to be made up of winding single-track streets, narrower and windier than even Wilfordshire's. Half-timbered houses, old churches, and medieval-looking towers completed the picture-perfect fairy-tale view.

The bedroom was up a second spiral staircase. The ceilings were lower here, and the spherical-shaped room was smaller than the one directly beneath it. The master bed was a queen-sized double-poster with net curtains all around it.

How romantic, Lacey thought, wryly.

Over to the side, the three camp beds had been set up and made with lots of pillows and extra blankets.

"These look comfy!" Tom said, sinking into one.

Frankie dive bombed the one beside him, sending an explosion of pillows into the air.

"I guess I'll take this one," Lacey said, reluctantly heading over to the bed shoved up against the shadiest wall, the furthest from Tom, and dumping her case on top of it.

"Where to first?" Naomi said, as she swirled out of the adjoining bathroom she'd just been inspecting.

Shirley picked up a tourist leaflet from the sideboard. "Looks like there's about fifty chic eateries to choose from." She looked at Tom. "Unless you're a golf man. There seem to be a lot of golf courses."

"Why don't we just go exploring first?" Lacey suggested. "Get a feel for the place?"

"There's a seafront pub!" Shirley exclaimed to Naomi, completely ignoring Lacey's suggestion.

Naomi hurried over to her mother and peered over her shoulder at the leaflet. "Ooh, look. *Through the old town walls lie the smugglers' lanes. Once a thoroughfare for pirates and their stolen treasure, this labyrinth maze of streets is now home to over one hundred boutiques and artisan jewelry stores.*" Her eyes glinted with excitement. "Let's go shopping!"

"Shopping?" Lacey repeated, incredulous. She pointed her finger out the window. "You want to shop when we could be going on a cliff-side ramble? Or visiting the medieval towers?"

"Or seeing the secret wartime tunnels," Frankie piped up, pointing at the picture on the front of Shirley's leaflet.

"Exactly!" Lacey exclaimed, pleased to have an ally.

Naomi grimaced. "But I *really* want to go shopping. You wouldn't let us shop for clothes in Wilfordshire, and I didn't bring anything appropriate for the weather."

Lacey looked her up and down. Her patterned gypsy skirt, strappy Gladiator sandals, and white spaghetti T seemed perfectly suited for the mild summer day as far as Lacey was concerned.

"We're in one of the most unique places of natural beauty in England," Lacey said. "It's filled with history. And you want to go *shopping?*"

Naomi shrugged. "I'm not feeling this jacket."

Shirley seemed to agree. "It is a bit last season. And I'd also love a pair of these boating shoes everyone's wearing."

"Typical," Lacey said. "You want the boating shoes but not to actually visit the ports and the boats? Or the maritime museum with a bronze age boat?"

Frankie looked extremely excited. "Bronze age boat?" he squealed.

Tom, slipping straight into Genial English Gentleman Mode, suggested, "Why don't we split up. You and Frankie go visit the museums or cliffs or whatever it is you feel like doing, and Shirley and Naomi can head to the smugglers' lanes for some retail therapy."

"What about you, Tom?" Frankie asked. "Will you come with us?"

"No, come with us," Shirley said. "I need to get to know my future son-in-law."

"Mom!" Lacey exclaimed, heat flushing into her face so quickly her ears burned.

"Oh, honestly," Shirley said dismissively. "If you don't snap him up someone else will."

"Someone like me," Naomi said, laughing heartily at her own joke.

But Lacey didn't see the funny side. Her family was playing tug-of-war with her boyfriend, and it looked like he was letting them win.

"We can meet back up here for a spot of lunch," Tom added.

"Typical man," Naomi said, rolling her eyes. "He has no idea how long it will take us to shop."

"We'll meet back here for dinner," Shirley clarified, looking at her watch. "Six p.m. rendezvous?"

"What?" Lacey stammered.

That meant a whole day without Tom. It also meant an entire day entertaining Frankie. And as much as Lacey wanted to see the cliffs and the ocean and the maritime museum, she didn't know if she could cope with a young kid with a young kid's attention span.

"Dinner?" Tom repeated. For the first time he looked like he might have bitten off more than he could chew.

Feeling stubborn, Lacey folded her arms. "Okay," she said petulantly. "You guys go shopping. Me and Frankie are going to explore. And learn. And enrich our brains."

Yes, she was going against her own interests. But maybe the only way Tom would learn was through experience. After an entire day having his ear talked off while being used as a shopping bag mule for her mom and sister, he'd probably have enough of them for a lifetime.

"So we'll see you back here then?" Tom said, before adding a little hesitantly, "For . . . dinner."

"I can't wait to see what you cook for us!" Naomi gushed, as she waltzed out of the room, her gypsy skirt swirling around her.

Tom looked at Lacey with an expression of mild terror. Lacey just gave him a stubborn nod.

"Enjoy your day."

Lacey regretted it almost as soon as she and Frankie began their journey into town together. She felt anxious about being the responsible parental figure. It was a role her ex-husband, David, had tried to force upon her. One she'd resisted so much it eventually led to their divorce. Despite being the wrong side of thirty-five, she felt woefully underqualified for the responsibilities of keeping a small person safe, well, happy, and alive.

"So…" Lacey said stiltedly to Frankie when they reached the bottom of the road and the town lay ahead of them. "Where to first?"

"The war tunnels," Frankie exclaimed excitedly.

Lacey pulled out the tourist leaflet she'd taken from the lighthouse inn and searched for the tunnels. "Shoot! They had to close this summer for essential maintenance work. Anywhere else you want to go?"

"A museum would be good," Frankie said.

"Great idea." Lacey checked the map. "Okay, the maritime museum is only open on the weekends, but there's a whole bunch of art museums over here. Do you like art?"

Frankie didn't look convinced. "I guess."

"Cool. So…" She studied the map. "They're kind of far out. But that's okay, we can just take a bus." She switched to her cell phone, checking the local bus company's timetable. "It takes an HOUR?" she exclaimed. Then, remembering the beady-eyed, expectant young boy looking at her for guidance, she coughed and added, "Which is fine. Obviously. And it's just a little walk from there." She looked at the map again. "A little…half-hour walk."

"Don't worry, Auntie Lacey," Frankie said, sounding a little glum. "We don't have to go. I'd get carsick on a bus for an hour anyway."

Lacey lowered the map, disappointed she had fallen at the first child-care hurdle: keep them happy. "I'm sorry, kiddo."

Beneath his messy auburn curls, Frankie flashed her an insulted look. "Kiddo?"

Lacey scratched her neck. "I guess you're not really a kiddo anymore, are you?"

"I'm eight," Frankie replied, in a tone that implied eight years old was so obviously more mature than seven years old.

Beyond the foot in height he'd acquired over the last few months, and the sprouting "big teeth" that looked far too large for his mouth, Frankie's chaotic energy also seemed to have diminished. He seemed more focused. Still a live-wire, but a little more channeled with it. If Lacey could find something to direct him toward, she might just make it through the day.

The first store on the corner was a candy store, the type with glass jars filled with colorful candy. *Ye Olde Sweet Shoppe*, its sign proclaimed, just in case there was any doubt as to what it was all about.

"Is eight too old for candy?" Lacey asked Frankie, pointing to the store.

"Heck no!" he cried.

Lacey chuckled, and they headed inside.

The decor was just like an Edwardian-era candy store, complete with black-and-white-tiled flooring and dark wooden shelves. The candies were displayed in big glass jars. Powder pink bonbons, buttercup yellow bonbons, spearmint bonbons, lemon sherbets... It reminded Lacey of the first shop she'd ventured into in Wilfordshire. Magical. Quaint. Idyllic.

"Gobstoppers!" Frankie exclaimed, looking at a jar of golf-ball-sized, licorice-flavored gobstoppers that Lacey couldn't help but see as choking hazards.

From behind the long counter, a man in a white apron came over to serve them. He had a thin moustache twirled up at both ends, a daring style Lacey had only ever seen sported by inner city hipsters. He was clearly very committed to the ye olde style illusion the store was trying to emulate.

"Hello, young sir," he said with old-fashioned aplomb. "I'm Arnold, your confectioner for today. And what can I interest you in?"

Frankie seemed delighted by the whole act. He peered down into the glass display cabinet, his eyes wide with excitement. "Auntie Lacey, it's arranged in the order they were invented!" he exclaimed.

"That's quite right, my eagle-eyed scallywag," Arnold continued. "We begin with the Turkish Delight from 1777. Then onto marshmallows, invented around 1850." He moved along the row, gesturing with his hand to the pretty displays of candy. "The nineteenth century's offerings of toffee, fudge, Kendal mint cake, peanut brittle, jellybeans, and wine gums, and here we have the first ever milk chocolate bar, created in 1875."

Frankie stared from the cabinet to Lacey and back again.

"Why don't we get two of each?" Lacey suggested. "Then we can eat them in date order, too."

Frankie nodded his agreement with the plan, and Arnold filled up pink-and-white-striped paper bags full to the brim with all their candies.

"Now we can say we went to a museum of sorts," Lacey joked as they left the store.

They strolled slowly along the streets, passing barbers and bookstores, nail bars and wine bars, savoring their candies as they went.

"Can we go in here?" Frankie asked.

He'd stopped outside a souvenir shop, but not the sort of tacky gaudy one Lacey was used to seeing. It was a tiny little store filled with unique handcrafted artworks, from greetings cards to posters, tote bags, coffee cups, and sweet little trinkets. They headed inside and started looking around.

A bright display of coasters caught Lacey's attention. The cute cartoons depicted everything British, from the Spice Girls to Harry Potter, the Beatles to Bowie. Next along were fridge magnets in the shape of speech bubbles, with cheeky British slang phrases like "Fancy a cuppa?", "Cheers mate!" and "Blimey!" Lacey couldn't resist; she had to get a "Bloody Hell" one for Gina, since she was so fond of saying it.

Frankie chose a notebook with seven cute cartoon corgis depicted on it.

Satisfied with their purchases, they headed back out into the sunny streets.

"Hey, look," Frankie said, his mouth and lips stained blue by the candy. "There's an antiques store over there, just like yours."

Lacey peered across the street. Frankie was right. There was a small brick building with large windows displaying antiques. Its dark green weathered sign proclaimed in cracked gold paint: *Forsythe's.*

"Shall we go inside?" Frankie suggested.

"You want to?" Lacey asked, a little surprised he was interested in old things.

"Yeah!" he said enthusiastically, grinning a sticky smile with his big goofy teeth. "I really liked exploring your store. And there might even be some Scottish stuff inside!"

"Maybe," Lacey said, touched that Frankie was showing even a semblance of interest in her passion.

Maybe this whole childcare thing wasn't so hard after all. Perhaps she was actually going to have a good time on her vacation.

Then again, Lacey thought, life had a funny way of throwing curve balls her way just when she thought everything was going well.

They crossed the street and headed inside.

Chapter Ten

Stepping inside the antiques store was like stepping through the enchanted mirror into Wonderland... if Wonderland was a dark, dusty, crammed store that smelled of engine grease, and where every nook and cranny was taken up with some peculiar object.

"Whoa!" Frankie exclaimed, turning around in circles. "This is nothing like your store, Auntie Lacey. There's so much stuff!"

He was right about that. While Lacey went to great pains to carefully curate her own merchandise—either by era, color, function, type, or room—this shop's owner had made next to no attempt to do so. Where Lacey was careful to stock only good-quality pieces to ensure her customers never ended up with something defective, this shop's owner had crammed it with a lot of shabby-looking bits of junk. The store made Lacey's look as minimalist as Taryn's boutique in comparison.

Lacey looked above her where nails hammered into the ceiling beams displayed all kinds of pots and pans hung next to tools and spare parts for cars. There seemed to be no logic to how anything had been displayed at all. A cardboard box filled with vintage buttons supported another cardboard box filled with jewelry, where worthless handcrafted plastic bead bracelets were mixed in with vintage pearl necklaces. There was a hat stand with bright yellow fisherman's macs and high visibility workman's jackets stuffed in right next to a genuine Letterman jacket and a 1960s tartan print cloak. The owner was clearly a hoarder who had no idea of the worth of any of the stock he was holding on to. The bric-a-brac and the vintage items were all mixed up together. It was the sort of place she'd probably find some amazing rare items... if she had a month to devote to the task.

Frankie became engrossed by a war-era children's magazine, and Lacey peered at a tall set of shelves by the window. Each shelf was stuffed with a random assortment of books, crockery, figurines, clocks, and ornaments. There was a very interesting accordion that looked as if it may have been a real Romanian one, though Lacey didn't have quite enough expertise to know for sure without calling Jack, her antique instrument contact. In front of the accordion was a gold Italian Rococo mantel clock, and a pair of matching Rococo candle holders, which would probably be of interest to her friend Percy, who had a fondness for the style. Lacey noticed the handwritten price tag attached to the candle holders said *three thousand pounds*. She whistled. That seemed steep, even to her partially trained eye.

"Auntie Lacey, look at this!" Frankie cried before she had a chance to inspect them further.

Lacey peered around. Frankie was nowhere to be seen. She'd lost him somewhere in the chaos.

A bolt of terror struck her. She couldn't lose her nephew the very first time she'd been given responsibility for him!

She shuffled through the stacks and piles and looming shelving units, until she maneuvered around a precarious-looking stack of novels and found Franke, crouched beside a tatty leather suitcase. He was sifting through the contents of a velvet pouch, making whatever was inside clink.

"What have you got there?" she asked, her racing heart slowing with relief.

"Coins," he said, peering up at her. He tipped them out on top of a worn leather suitcase. "Can you help me find out if any of them are Scottish?"

"There's nothing Scottish in there," a gruff voice said from the darkness.

Like some kind of ogre emerging from a swamp, a man slowly lumbered toward them. He was portly, with wiry white beard hairs sprouting haphazardly and in all directions from his chin. His T-shirt was too small, showing off a strip of pale white stomach beneath, which was as hairy as his chin. "Just some old coins," he said. "If you're lucky there'll be some halfpennies. Maybe even something Roman. Studdleton Bay has at least a hundred detectorists digging up the countryside and beaches searching for treasures." He scoffed disdainfully.

Lacey deduced that the man was the store's owner, though he seemed to exude hatred toward his chosen profession. He especially seemed disdainful of detectorists.

"What's a detectorist?" Frankie asked the shop clerk.

The man gave Frankie a look of contempt. Lacey bristled.

"They're the people who use metal detectors to search for old things made of metal," Lacey told him. "Like coins."

"Cool!" Frankie exclaimed. "Can we do that too?"

The shop owner scoffed. Lacey glared at him. Why was he being a jerk to a little kid?

"I should introduce myself," she said. "I'm Lacey. I have my own antiques store in Wilfordshire."

"Never heard of it," he barked, looking thoroughly disinterested.

"I didn't catch your name," Lacey said, trying her hardest to stay polite.

Without speaking, he pointed at his name tag. Desmond Forsythe.

"Well, Desmond," she said through gritted teeth. "Do you know where we might be able to hire a metal detector? My nephew Frankie has obviously taken an interest in the activity, and I'd like to nurture it."

"Why? So you can dig up the countryside with the rest of them?" he said scathingly. "Kid'll get bored in five seconds after he realizes it takes more than a lucky guess to actually find anything valuable. Once he has a bag full of beer tops and can pulls he'll give up. If you want to 'nurture his interests,' why don't you buy that bag of coins and a collector's manual and start there?"

Lacey was half tempted to march Frankie straight out of the surly man's store, but her nephew seemed utterly engrossed by the contents of the grab bag, and anything that stopped him talking about Scotland for a minute was worth it.

"We'll take the grab bag," she said, stiffly.

Desmond smiled nastily and snatched her money from her hand.

Lacey turned on her heel and marched out of the store. So much for making a new contact! She'd be happy to never see that terrible man again.

"I'm starving," Frankie said, as he and Lacey began their return journey to the lighthouse inn.

"Really? But you ate about a million candies today."

Frankie grinned. "Empty calories, Auntie Lacey. Honestly, you're old enough to know that by now."

Lacey smirked at Frankie's humor—not that she took kindly to being called old—but she did enjoy watching his little personality develop before her very eyes.

They reached the base of the lighthouse. Lacey unlocked the bright red door and entered.

"We're home!" she called up the winding staircase.

Frankie hushed her and pointed at the locked door to their left. Inside was the other guest apartment. So far, they hadn't heard a peep out of this other couple, and every time they'd passed, the door had been firmly shut.

Lacey pressed a finger to her lips and checked her watch. Though they were home an hour before dinner was due to be served, she'd expected Tom to have already begun cooking. He liked to take his time making a meal, to savor it.

She turned back to Frankie, who was depositing his shoes by the door. "Looks like no one else is home yet."

Frankie neatened his shoes beside the welcome mat. "That means we won't be having dinner for aaaages."

Lacey realized she was going to have to distract him. Again. "Hey. Why don't we see what treasure we found?" She pointed at the velvet pouch bulging in Frankie's pocket.

Her nephew's eyes widened with excitement. "Okay!"

They went up the creaking wooden steps, winding around in spirals until they reached the floor with the living room. Then they sat on the floor either side of the coffee table, and Frankie tipped the grab bag up, depositing its contents on the table. A bunch of coins fell from it with the dull tinkle of thin, flimsy, old metal.

Frankie began sifting through it. "Pennies. Pennies. Pennies." He looked up at Lacey and stuck out his bottom lip. "They're all the same. Just a bunch of grimy old pennies."

"That's a shame," Lacey said. "I was hoping there'd be something interesting in there. Still, how many of your friends have a collection of old Roman pennies..." Her voice trailed away as her attention was drawn to something shiny buried in the pile of dull pennies, only barely visible. She reached forward and plucked it out. Holding it up to the light, Lacey gasped.

"What's that?" Frankie asked with wonder, his eyes transfixed on the large shiny coin in Lacey's fingertips.

"I think..." Lacey said, turning the coin in her fingers so the light caught it and made it glitter, "...it's gold."

Frankie's mouth dropped open. "Gold?" he repeated. "Real gold?"

"I can't be one hundred percent certain," Lacey said, though her heart was starting to hammer with excitement. "I'm not an expert on coins."

It was an imperfect circle, so made before industrialization. The edges were beveled, so the metal was soft enough to have been misshaped over years buried beneath the earth. She turned the coin over to inspect the head side. To her astonishment, it depicted the very distinct profile of a Roman emperor.

"It can't be..." Lacey murmured.

"Can't be what?" Frankie asked. He started bouncing up and down. "What can't it be, Auntie Lacey?"

Lacey couldn't quite believe her eyes. If this was the real deal and not a replica, then she was holding a Roman-era gold coin.

"Are we rich?" Frankie asked, getting to his feet now. "Auntie Lacey, are we rich?"

His excitement was making it harder for Lacey to temper her own. Her work in appraising had told her if it looked too good to be true, then it probably wasn't true. Without the eye of an expert in the field, she wouldn't know for certain. Thinking rationally, it was more likely to be a replica, especially since it was all mixed up in a grab bag of other assorted, non-valuable coins. But some other instinct was telling her it was real.

"We'd need to get it valued to know for certain," she told Frankie.

Frankie started hopping up and down. "Then let's go and get it valued!"

"We can't," Lacey said. "Not now. I don't know any appraisers in Studdleton Bay. I wouldn't even know where to start looking for one." Returning to Forsythe's was out of the question. The store clerk had made it perfectly clear he wasn't the helpful type.

"What about the inn lady?" Frankie suggested. He was flapping his arms now, like some kind of excited bird.

"Helen Ashworth?" Lacey said, thinking of the inn owner in her red barn. "That's not a bad idea. And we have an hour before dinner anyway."

She could feel herself getting caught up in Frankie's excitement, and she tried hard to calm her own. That didn't stop her from hurrying down the lighthouse steps, leaping out into the courtyard, and racing along the path with Frankie to the reception area in the bright red barn.

Helen looked up from the counter as they clattered inside, panting. Her eyebrows rose upward toward her mousy brown hairline, held back by its purple velour headband.

"Is everything okay?" she asked, looking concerned.

"Yes, we wanted to ask you for a recommendation," Lacey said, still quite out of breath from the sprint.

"Eating out or takeaway?" Helen said, reaching for a stack of take-out pamphlets.

Lacey shook her head. "Not food. We need a recommendation for an antiques valuer."

Helen paused. A line of confusion appeared between her brows. "I'm sorry, a what now?"

"An antiques valuer!" Frankie squealed, his excitement clearly too much for him to contain any longer.

Lacey hushed him gently.

"Have you tried the antiques store in town?" Helen asked, sounding perplexed. "Forsythe's."

"Not him," Lacey blurted, failing to contain her own disdain toward the surly man. "Is there anyone else?"

"A different man ran the store before him," Helen said, pursing her lips. "He's very elderly though, so I can't be sure he's still working in the field. His house is up by the church on the hill, if he isn't retired by now."

Lacey and Frankie exchanged an excited glance.

"Thanks!" Lacey cried.

She and Frankie ran out of the reception, leaving a baffled-looking Helen behind.

Lacey's legs ached from trying to keep up with Frankie as he marched up the hill with speed. The little church at the top was like a beacon they were heading for.

Once they reached it, they found it was actually part of a larger building, a terrace of one-story cottages arranged in a rectangle shape, with a square of grass in the middle like a shared courtyard.

"Almshouse," Frankie said, reading a sign attached to the wrought iron railings that made up the final side of the rectangle. "What does that mean?"

"Ah yes," Lacey told him. "There's a lot of these in the UK. They have a bunch of them in London. I've seen them when Gina and I travel there for work. They were built by the English church for their parishioners hundreds of years ago. The church sits in the middle, and everyone who lives in the house is expected to attend daily services, as well as maintain a very high level of Christian behavior."

"Which one is the appraiser's house?" Frankie asked.

Lacey scanned them. There were ten houses in total, two either side of the central church, and three on each arm of the rectangle.

"I don't know," Lacey said.

"Let's try them all," Frankie said, pushing open the gate.

"Wait, Frankie!" Lacey cried, starting to feel some hesitation. They couldn't just march up to a stranger's house and knock on their door, could they? It all seemed a bit brash.

But she didn't really get a chance to mull it over because Frankie was already up the path and knocking enthusiastically on the first door.

The door opened, and a little old man peered out. He was wearing a dark green knitted jumper that hung to his thighs. His white beard was patchy in places, as if poorly maintained. Lacey felt bad for having disturbed him.

"Hi, I'm Frankie!" her nephew announced right away. "Are you an antiques valuer?"

The man looked surprised to find a ginger-haired American boy on his doorstep. "Yes," he said cautiously, like he wasn't entirely sure he should be admitting to such a thing.

"You are?" Frankie asked, grinning. He looked over his shoulder at Lacey and exclaimed, "Auntie Lacey, I found him!"

Lacey could feel her cheeks warming. She hurried up the path to join Frankie by his side.

"I'm so sorry to disturb you," she said to the man. "My name is Lacey. This is my nephew, Frankie. I own an antiques store, and was told you may be able to help me with valuing something."

"Do you work at Forsythe's?" he asked. His voice was croaky and thin.

Lacey shook her head. "No. My store is in Wilfordshire. We're just here on vacation."

"Wilfordshire? What state is that in?"

Lacey shook her head. "Oh, no. It's not in America. I live in England. Devon."

By the confused expression on his face, Lacey wasn't sure if he was in full possession of his faculties. But he nodded and shuffled back from the door. "Come on in then."

Frankie punched the air triumphantly and hopped inside the man's home. Lacey, still uncertain about taking her nephew into a strange man's home, went inside nonetheless.

Though the decor of the cottage was aged, harkening back to the 1970s era of brown, orange, and paisley, the relics decorating it were numerous and staggeringly beautiful. The shelves displayed Chinese vases in the famous black lacquered Qing dynasty style. The walls were adorned with antique oil paintings in gold-leaf frames. The house was like a testament to the man's career in antiques, and Lacey felt inspired to one day make Crag Cottage look just as beautiful, to collect just as many wonderful, unique items to display all over her home.

"Do you want tea?" the man called over his shoulder.

"Why don't I make it?" Lacey asked, not wanting to trouble him any more than they already had.

"Do you know how?" the man replied, sounding surprised.

"I've been living here long enough," Lacey said with a chuckle.

They entered his kitchen, which would have been spacious enough for the three of them had it not been for the vast amounts of antiques on displays. In fact, as Lacey looked around, she saw that every single item inside the kitchen was an antique, from the French farmhouse dining table in pale elm, to the rustic pine double-drawer butcher's block, upon which sat a real Victorian-era egg cupboard large enough for at least two dozen eggs. She counted five bookshelves in a row against one wall, and every single space on every single shelf displayed a unique, exotic ornament; a golden monkey statue, a woven basket in bamboo, a Venetian carnival mask, a town crier's bell, a gorgeous silver crucifix, a crystal cake stand, a pair of cast iron giraffes. Somehow they all worked perfectly well together. The old man had curated them perfectly, so nothing looked out of place. It was the type of skill Lacey was still cultivating in herself.

Even the flooring was unique. It was made from a vast mosaic of tiles in cream and gray, reminding her of an Old Roman road she'd seen on display in a museum in Exeter. The intricate design must have taken hours of work to create.

Through a thick layer of dust on a framed certificate on the wall, Lacey read the man's name: Martin Ormsby. She thought briefly of Martina the house martin above her porch in Wilfordshire, and wondered how the bird and her chicks were getting on. Hopefully, annoying Taryn!

Lacey quickly found the kettle (a vintage Delonghi in duck egg blue), the teapot (a vintage Brown Betty), and the teabags (stored in a battered, vintage post-war PG Tips tin). She set about brewing them a pot, realizing the experience was ten times more enjoyable thanks to the beautiful antiques she got to handle while making it. She became yet more determined to make Crag Cottage the same.

Frankie took a seat on the small table by the window, and Martin sat opposite him.

"Where are you staying while you're on vacation?" he asked, genially.

"The lighthouse," Frankie said. "It's the other side of town, up the hill. Do you know it?"

"No, I don't think I do," Martin said.

"Well, the woman there recommended you," Frankie continued. "When we asked if she knew any valuers."

Martin shrugged. "My memory isn't what it used to be."

While Lacey made the tea, Frankie removed the grab bag from his pocket and poured the contents out onto the table.

"Roman coins," Martin croaked straight away. "Goodness, I've seen many of these in my time. They're not particularly valuable, though some of the ones in better condition can fetch up to twenty pounds. But listen, sonny, they're an excellent item to collect. People pay more for collections, for starters, and as years pass, they'll become more and more valuable. So take care of them."

Frankie pushed the coins with his fingertips until the bright, shiny gold one was exposed.

Martin's gaze fell upon it, and he gasped.

Lacey came over with the teapot and mugs. "That's what we're here for you to value."

"My, oh my," Martin said. He picked up the coin with his shaking, wizened hands and held it just an inch away from his nose. He squinted. "Now that is rare. Very rare indeed."

"It's gold, isn't it?" Lacey asked, hopefully. Her anticipation was almost too much to handle, so she distracted herself with pouring the tea.

"It's gold, all right," Martin said, in his slow, raspy voice. "The emperor on its face is Emperor Nero. That makes this around two thousand years old."

Lacey's hands started to shake as she moved on to the next cup.

Frankie whistled his astonishment. "How much is it worth?" he said, asking the question Lacey herself was too nervous to.

What Martin Ormsby said next almost made Lacey drop the teapot mid-pour.

"In the right hands," he said, "this coin could fetch six figures."

CHAPTER ELEVEN

Frankie skipped down Martin Ormsby's path, much to the bemusement of a little old lady pruning a bush in the almshouse's central square.

"What does six figures mean, Auntie Lacey?" he asked.

"It means..." Lacey stammered. "It means...hundreds of thousands of pounds."

Frankie's mouth dropped open. "Hundreds of thousands of pounds? That sounds like a lot!"

He skipped through the gate of the almshouse back onto the street. "How many times would I be able to ride the Jacobite Steam Train through the Scottish Highlands?" he asked. "More than ten?"

"More like a thousand," Lacey said, but she couldn't share his enthusiasm. "Frankie. We can't keep it."

Frankie stopped spinning and stared at her. He blinked. "What? Why?"

"Because it wouldn't be right," Lacey said. "Desmond Forsythe can't have known it was in there. It must've been a mistake."

"But...but finders keepers," Frankie stated.

Lacey shook her head. "That doesn't work on the playground and it definitely doesn't work in real life. I'm sorry, Frankie, but it wouldn't be right. We'll have to return it."

"But..." Frankie began again. His little kid brain was obviously struggling to compute Lacey's grown-up sense of morality. "I want to go on the Jacobite Steam Train."

He looked like he was about to cry, and Lacey couldn't help but feel compassion. She crouched a little so they were head height. "But maybe Desmond Forsythe wants to go on the Jacobite Steam Train too. And maybe he's wanted to his whole life but never had enough money. And he's been working hard and saving up and now, finally, he has this gold coin. If he sells it, he'll be able to afford the train ride ... but then he realizes he's lost the coin. Imagine how that would feel."

To Lacey's surprise, Frankie's face immediately softened with understanding. "I guess I have more time to work hard and save up the money than Desmond Forsythe does." He nodded slowly, as if making up his mind. "Okay. We can return it."

Lacey smiled. Maybe she wasn't so bad at this parenting malarkey.

She checked her watch. "You know, the antiques store will be closed now, so we'll have to wait until tomorrow to take it back. Which means we can spend the whole evening at the lighthouse playing with it, pretending to be rich Roman emperors."

Frankie grinned.

They returned to the lighthouse. Through the window of the barn, Helen's eyes followed them as they passed. She looked just as perplexed as she had when they'd rushed out. Lacey gave her a jovial wave. Curiously, she ducked back away from the window and into the safety of the shadows. Lacey frowned, confused by her behavior, but shrugged it off and continued on to the lighthouse.

But when she opened the door, everything inside was silent. No sound from upstairs, none from behind the green door of the guests staying on the ground floor. The others still hadn't returned.

Lacey fired off a message to Tom. *Where are you?*

Her phone pinged in response. It was Tom.

The Bluebird Inn, waiting for you two.

Lacey frowned. *I thought we were having dinner here.*

Tom's reply came a moment later. *Oh. Naomi was supposed to message you. There was a change of plan.*

Of course, Lacey thought, exhaling slowly. Tom obviously didn't know her sister well enough to know never to leave anything important to Naomi.

"Hey, Frankie," she said, putting on a bright tone that was about a mile away from how she actually felt. The boy looked up at her from where he was unlacing his shoes on the welcome mat. "Looks like there's been a change in dinner plans. Mom, Gran, and Tom found a place in town they want to eat at instead. The Bluebird Inn. Sounds nice. Is that okay with you?"

"Sure," Frankie said. "What about my Roman coin? Can I bring it with me?"

"Better not," Lacey told him. "It would be terrible if we lost it. How about you choose a special hiding place in the lighthouse to keep the grab bag safe?"

Frankie's face lit up at the mention of a secret hiding place. "I know just the place! The trunk of the elephant figurine!" He was off like a rocket to hide their velvet bag of treasure.

Lacey couldn't help but smile to herself. She'd thought spending time with Frankie would be draining and difficult, just as Naomi always made it out to be. But it had been fun. More than fun. It had been fulfilling. Satisfying. It had felt important, like everything she said and how she handled things mattered. For the first time in her life, Lacey thought, *Maybe becoming a mother wouldn't be so bad after all...*

The restaurant was a quaint little place, with a low ceiling and creaky floorboards. The building must've been hundreds of years old. The walls weren't straight, bulging out in places as if made in an age before measuring tapes and spirit levels.

They found Tom, Naomi, and Shirley at a large round wooden table waiting for them, surrounded by an array of shopping bags. Lacey felt a little tug of anger in her chest that Naomi had failed to keep them abreast of the changing plans, but then she remembered how fun her day with Frankie had actually been, and the feeling quickly passed.

"How was your shopping trip?" Lacey asked, as she gave Tom a peck on the cheek and took the spare seat next to him.

"Great!" Naomi exclaimed before Tom even had a chance to open his mouth. "There were so many cute little boutiques, and because I have no idea what the exchange rate is, I didn't have to feel guilty splurging."

"I'm not sure that's how it works..." Lacey began.

But her sister didn't hear because she was still talking excitedly over her. "Check out my new jacket!"

She started rustling around in her bags, before pulling out a denim jacket that looked remarkably similar to the one she was already wearing.

"It's gorgeous," Lacey commented. She'd worked out many years ago to take the path of least resistance when it came to Naomi and her questionable choices.

"I got some boating shoes," Shirley said, kicking her foot up in the air and wiggling it.

"Also lovely, Mom," Lacey said. "But maybe keep your feet off the table."

"I'm not touching," Shirley said, completely missing the point.

Lacey turned to Tom. "Well, this is a nice choice. Did you pick it?"

"I did," Naomi butted in, again robbing Tom of the chance to actually utter a syllable. "I thought Tom could do with a night off from the cooking. Honestly, Lacey, from what he's been telling me, it sounds like you treat him like a proper 1950s housewife."

Frankie giggled.

Lacey opened her mouth in mock offense. "I do not! He offers to cook because he's better at it than me. And then he likes to wash up after so I don't scratch his precious pans and utensils."

Tom chuckled at her gentle teasing. "I've got to take care of my tools. They're my livelihood."

"Just don't let her get too comfy," Shirley commented. "Lacey as a kept woman would be insufferable."

"Mom!" Lacey exclaimed, her offense genuine this time. "I'm far from being a kept woman. Have you already forgotten my store? You know, the business I built myself from the ground up. The place I toil at day and night, where I earned enough money to buy my own home?"

Shirley waved the comment away and went back to admiring her new boating shoes. Lacey sat back in her chair and crossed her arms.

Kept woman . . . she thought with irritation.

She looked at Naomi. "What made you choose this place?" she asked, trying to make polite conversation, even though she'd said it between her teeth.

"You refused to let me have a pint of bitters in Wilfordshire," Naomi said. "And I asked Tom to find somewhere that sold them. He pointed out this place. Then I said how you'd told me Frankie was too young to go inside pubs and Tom told me that wasn't true at all."

Darn, Lacey thought. She'd been caught. "Well, the bitters thing is true. No one calls it a 'pint of bitters.'"

"We'll see about that," Naomi replied.

Just then, a server came over with a tray of drinks. "One red wine," he said, placing a glass in front of Shirley, "and two pints of bitter."

"Ha!" Naomi said triumphantly as a large glass tankard filled with amber-colored liquid was placed in front of her. "See."

Lacey's cheeks warmed. She knew the server was only being accommodating of the brash American and her tourist terminology. She wanted to apologize to him for it, but he was obviously used to it. So she held her tongue, choosing to avoid that particular battle with Naomi today.

Naomi lifted her heavy pint glass to her lips and took a sip. Her face soured. "That is disgusting."

Lacey quickly looked up at the server and loudly spoke over Naomi before she embarrassed her any further. "Can I get a dry white wine please? And a cola for the kid. I mean, the young gentleman."

Frankie nodded, satisfied.

The server wrote down their orders. "And are you ready to order your food?"

Lacey quickly scanned the menu. It was full of traditional English dishes with strange-sounding names.

"I'll have the bangers and mash, please," Lacey said.

Frankie giggled. "And I'll have the toad in the hole!"

The two of them fell about laughing, earning themselves a disdainful frown from Naomi.

"Shepherd's pie for me," Tom said, folding his menu shut and handing it to the server.

"I'll try the bubble and squeak," Shirley said.

Everyone looked at Naomi, who was still scanning the menu. "Can I just, like, get something healthy? Everything here is so starchy. Pastry. Bread. Pastry. Bread. I just don't get why everyone's so obsessed with pastry and bread." She looked over her menu at Tom. "No offense."

Tom held up a hand to indicate he'd taken none, but Lacey slunk down in her chair a little because really the person who'd been offended was the server and Naomi barely seemed to realize he was there.

"We do a garden salad," the server told her.

"Yeah," Naomi said, sounding less than thrilled. "I guess that'll have to do. But no dressing. Or onion. And I want a grilled chicken breast on the side."

"Chicken?" Frankie said, sounding alarmed. "Like Trixie?"

Naomi gave her son a look as she thrust her menu back at the server. "Do I need to remind you that your favorite food is chicken drumsticks? You've eaten plenty of Trixies in your time, and a whole bunch of Rosies too."

The server's eyes widened.

Lacey coughed into her hand, embarrassed.

Shirley leaned her torso across the table inelegantly, so she was closer to the server. "Don't worry, we're not serial killers, we're just staying on a farm. All the chickens have names. Trixie. Rosie. What else? Helen."

"Helen's the owner!" Frankie bellowed, starting to giggle.

Shirley flapped her hand dismissively and took a deep glug from her wine glass.

The server nodded slowly, looking bemused. "Can I get you anything else?"

"Nah," Naomi said flippantly.

Lacey squirmed. "That's everything, thank you," she said in the most polite voice she could muster, hoping it might make up for her family's behavior.

The server left with their orders and a confused look on his face.

Tom took a sip from his tankard of bitter ale and sighed in satisfaction. His reaction was a million miles away from Naomi's. "We went to a great gallery earlier," he said as he placed his glass on top of his toucan-sporting beer mat. "Didn't we, ladies?"

Shirley giggled. Naomi smirked. Lacey felt her skin crawl. It wasn't that she disliked her mother and sister, per se, but the differences that already existed between them seemed to have turned into a chasm since Lacey's move to England. And it was she who had changed, Lacey realized. Mom and Naomi were the same fast-talking, on-the-go New Yorkers they always had been. It was she who'd slowed down, quieted down, and it struck her more in that moment than it ever had before.

As Shirley gushed over the oil paintings she'd seen today, the server returned with their respective meals. Lacey's bangers and mash was very beautifully presented; the creamy white potatoes were piled into a perfect mound, with glistening sausages poking out of it in pleasing angles, like some kind of food art.

The gravy came in a separate dish, a gorgeous white porcelain gravy boat that would look lovely on her chinaware shelf at Crag Cottage. She recalled Martin Ormsby's antique shelves and doubled down on her resolve to start decorating her own home in a beautiful way when she got back from vacation.

"That looks disgusting," Naomi said, frowning at Frankie's toad in the hole, which Lacey saw was a large soft pastry the size of his plate, with sausages baked right into it. "I can't believe Brits make sausages out of toads."

Lacey burst out laughing. "It's not made of toad! That's just the name! They're normal pork sausages."

Naomi didn't look thrilled at Lacey's outburst. "Well, the French eat frog's legs," she said gruffly. "Stop laughing at me like I'm an idiot."

"Fair point," Lacey said, holding her hands up in truce. But her shoulders still shook with laughter.

She took a fork full of mash and sampled the mixture of cream, butter, and background suggestion of chives. Mixed with the tangy, bittersweet, red onion gravy—with just a hint of red wine—Lacey's taste buds were in heaven. Then she tried the sausage and was delighted by the perfect ratio of pork to fat to juices.

Just then, Lacey felt a tugging on her sleeve. It was Frankie.

"Look, look," he was saying, pointing into the restaurant. "That man has ginger hair like me!"

"Frankie," Naomi snapped. "Don't point, it's rude."

"But Mom, I think he might be a real Scottish man. I heard him say something earlier and it sounded like he had an accent."

Naomi rolled her eyes. "Frankie. Please can you talk about something else? Anything else?"

Frankie huffed and folded his arms. He flopped back in his chair, looking grumpy.

"What did you do today with Auntie Lacey?" Naomi prompted.

But it was too late. Frankie was in a mood.

"We found a rare, valuable Roman-era coin," he mumbled.

"A coin?" Naomi asked. "Like in a museum?"

"No," he said testily. "Like in an antiques shop. We bought it and Auntie Lacey took me to an appraisers' house who told us it's super old and valuable."

All eyes turned to Lacey. She put down her fork and coughed.

"It's true," she said.

"How valuable are we talking?" Shirley asked, her eyes glinting with excitement.

"Six million pounds," Frankie said.

Shirley's mouth dropped open.

Lacey quickly shook her head. "He's exaggerating. It was valued as potentially fetching up to six figures. Not six million."

"Six figures!" Naomi screeched loud enough to draw the attention of the couple at the next table. She looked like Lacey had just told her she'd won the lottery. In a way, she sort of just had.

"Lacey," Tom said breathlessly, "that's amazing. That's life-changing. Think of all the things you can do."

Lacey shook her head, halting everyone before they got even more carried away. "The coin was sold to me by accident inside a grab bag of coins. I have to return it."

"WHAT?" Naomi cried, squeezing her fork in her fist.

Lacey leaned back in her chair just in case her sister got so worked up she jabbed her with it.

"You're returning it?" Tom asked softly. He was managing to stay neutral, though there was an edge in his tone Lacey was perceptive enough to pick up on.

"There's no way the owner of the store knew how valuable it was," Lacey said. "Keeping it for myself would be immoral."

"But you bought it fair and square!" Naomi continued, seemingly becoming even more incensed. "Whatever happened to finders keepers?"

Frankie piped up. "It doesn't work on the playground, and it doesn't work here."

"Exactly," Lacey said, happy to hear him repeat the wisdom she'd imparted on him earlier. "I'm not a twelve-year-old. I'm a professional in an industry with a reputation to maintain. I have to behave accordingly. If I made the same mistake, I'd be absolutely devastated."

"Only if you found out," Shirley said. "Didn't you say it was mixed up in a grab bag?"

Naomi clutched at the lifeline. "Right! You should hold on to it for at least a few days and see what happens. The owner might not even know it's missing."

Their scheming left a sour taste in Lacey's mouth. Giving back a valuable coin was hard enough without her family guilt tripping her over it.

"Can we please drop the subject?" Lacey said.

She took a sip of wine and averted her gaze from her family. Only for it to fall on none other than Desmond Forsythe.

He was standing in the doorway of the restaurant, having literally just walked in. He looked extremely out of place standing there with his big pot belly and angry scowling face. It was such an incongruous surprise, for a moment Lacey wasn't sure if she'd just invented him because she'd been talking about him. But the unmistakable pot belly, the sprouting chin and neck hairs, it was Desmond Forsythe, all right, standing in the Bluebird Inn restaurant like an apparition she'd materialized with her mind.

He appeared to be looking for someone. And he did not look happy. His scowl was even more pronounced than it had been when she'd met him earlier. Lacey felt terrible for whomever he was looking for; it seemed as if they were about to get an ear lashing!

At which point his gaze fell to her. The glint of evil in his eye made Lacey go cold all over. She realized with sudden dread that *she* was the person he was looking for! She was the poor so-and-so about to get an ear lashing!

"You!" Desmond bellowed, projecting his voice the whole way across the restaurant.

The general hubbub immediately ceased, as if someone had pressed the mute button, and in one perfectly synchronized swell of movement, every single head turned and stared at her.

Lacey felt her throat tighten.

"Uh-oh," Naomi said, covering her mouth with her napkin. "Looks like the loonies have been let out for the night."

There was no time to scold her for being rude, because Desmond was starting to approach, shoving his way through the tables, elbowing diners in his haste to get to Lacey. His fury was focused right on her.

"You! YOU! You bloody thief!" he screamed.

"Is he talking to us?" Tom said in a hushed tone, as he looked over his shoulder and realized there was no one else this stranger could be yelling at.

Shirley looked affronted.

"Not us," Lacey said stiffly. "Me."

None of the others had had any contact with Desmond Forsythe but her and Frankie, and she had a sneaking suspicion she knew exactly what was going on. Somehow, Desmond had found out about the coin he'd accidentally sold Lacey. Clearly gossip traveled as fast in Studdleton Bay as it did in Wilfordshire. And rather than speaking to Lacey about it rationally like a mature grown-up, Desmond had decided to make a scene and humiliate her, like some kind of oversized bloated baby.

Lacey put her wine glass down and stood, racking her brains for a way to defuse the situation.

"Can I help you, Desmond?" she asked, mustering her calmest voice despite the fact her heart was pounding.

Desmond drew up in front of her, anger smoldering in his eyes. "Can you help?" he repeated in a demeaning, sneering voice. "Don't play stupid, lady. You know exactly why I'm here!" He pointed his finger right in her face and declared to the silently stunned restaurant, "This woman is a thief!"

Tom flew to his feet, throwing his napkin onto his plate with such force it made his knife and fork clatter. "Now hang on a minute!"

Naomi's mouth dropped open, though there was a hint of intrigue in her eyes; she loved a good drama, after all. Frankie slunk lower into his seat, looking terrified that Desmond would turn his fury on him next if he noticed he was there.

"Tom," Lacey said in a low, firm voice. She pressed her hand gently to his chest. "Please let me handle this."

The last thing she needed right now was for Tom to square up to Desmond. As sweet as it was that he wanted to protect her honor, she was also pretty confident it would be better if she handled it her own way.

"Desmond, why don't you take a seat and we can discuss what the problem is," she said, hearing the tremble in her voice and hoping he didn't.

"Sit with you? A con artist? A deceiver? A thief?"

Desmond's booming voice carried all the way around the restaurant. On the next table over from them, the ginger-haired man and his female companion craned their heads to get a better view, like this was some kind of play at the theater. Over by the bar, the staff were starting to congregate, as if trying to work out when it would be best for them to intervene.

Lacey didn't much like being called names, but she knew reacting in any way would simply fuel the fire.

"I can assure you, there's just been a mix-up," she said, staying as calm as possible. "A misunderstanding."

Desmond's voice reached a fever pitch. "A misunderstanding? Is that what you call shoplifting?"

There was an audible intake of breath from the crowd of spectators.

"Now look, that's not what happened," Lacey said, shaking her head. He was going way too far now by implying she'd deliberately taken the coin from his store. "I didn't steal anything."

"He means the coin, Auntie Lacey," Frankie piped up. "The one we found in the grab bag."

Lacey's chest sank. She knew Frankie had only been trying to help, but his words were the accelerant to Desmond's argument.

"Ha!" Desmond screeched triumphantly. "The boy admits it! Did you all hear that?" He looked over his shoulder at the entire watching restaurant. "The little brat just admitted they stole my coin!"

Now it was Naomi's turn to become incensed. She leapt up so abruptly her chair screeched across the floorboards before falling back with a crash. "Don't you dare call my kid a brat!"

Desmond turned his nasty glare on her. "So you're the one responsible for this horrible little urchin? Why don't you act like a mother and get your kid to give me back my property!"

Naomi's face went beet-red. "How DARE you?!" she screamed.

She looked like she was just about ready to scratch his eyes out with her fingernails. Luckily Tom was in the way, and he took a side step to block her from launching an attack.

"Leave my nephew out of this," Lacey said to Desmond. "I'm the one who bought the grab bag. I found the coin inside. Nothing was stolen."

"A likely story!" Desmond spat in return. "You think anyone here will believe for a second that you 'bought' the coin? That it 'just happened' to be in the grab bag? Or is it more likely that you saw the coin and slipped it in the grab bag! Are you proud of yourself for conning an honest man out of his livelihood?"

Lacey was losing her patience now. She'd had every intention to return Desmond's property to him, and yet he'd come in all guns blazing, insulting her, insulting her family, publicly demeaning and belittling her, and now he was outright lying to defame her! Thanks to his terrible behavior, Lacey felt attacked. And when she felt attacked, she got stubbornly defensive.

"I think you'll find that it was your own negligence that led to this whole situation in the first place," she said, coolly. "I found the coin inside a grab bag, one I bought fair and square. Maybe you should check the contents of the grab bags *before* you sell them?"

It was, quite obviously, the wrong thing to say. Lacey knew it the minute the words were out of her mouth. Desmond's face turned a horrible shade of red like he was about to blow an artery. But she wasn't going to just stand there and be bullied. And she definitely wasn't going to give the coin back to him now after all this!

The wait staff came hurrying over, clearly deciding it was time to intervene. They created a physical barrier between Desmond and Lacey and her family.

"Sir, you need to leave," their server said.

"Me leave?" Desmond screamed. "She's the criminal!"

Shirley, now protected by a barrier of human bodies, stood. "How dare you!" she cried.

A shouting match ensued, with Desmond on one side being herded to the door by a line of wait staff, screeching obscenities, and Lacey's family on the other side shouting retorts.

"I'll call the police!" Desmond screamed.

"Possession is nine-tenths of the law!" Lacey retorted.

"I'll sue!" Desmond cried.

"Get lost, you big creep!" Naomi yelled.

"You'll be hearing from my lawyer!" Desmond finished, before the waiters hustled him all the way out the door of the restaurant.

As silence fell, Lacey could hear her heart pounding in her ears. She could feel every single pair of eyes in the restaurant staring at her, including Shirley and Naomi, who were comforting a very upset-looking Frankie.

So much for her family embarrassing her, she'd been the one to bring the embarrassment all by herself! She sank down into her seat, wishing the ground would swallow her up.

CHAPTER TWELVE

Lacey was still fuming from her encounter with Desmond by the time they made it back to the lighthouse inn. It didn't help that Frankie had spent the entire walk home lecturing Lacey about how immoral it was for her to keep the coin, echoing back the lesson she'd imparted on him earlier that day.

She kicked her shoes off at the door so hard they went pinging into the door of the downstairs guest.

Lacey winced. But from the other side, all was silent. Hopefully, they'd not been disturbed, though Lacey still hadn't seen any signs of there being anyone in there in the first place.

"Lacey, calm down," Shirley said, as she trudged up the stairs after her daughter.

"Calm down?" Lacey fumed. "Did you hear what he said to me!"

"I think the whole town heard what he said to you," Tom joked.

They filed into the living room.

"Where is this coin anyway?" Naomi asked.

Lacey sank onto the sofa with a huff. "I don't know. Frankie hid it somewhere. Frankie? Where are you?"

She craned her head over the back of the sofa to see Frankie over by the shelf of books and figurines. He was crouching down, moving a metal cast elephant aside.

"Um . . . Auntie Lacey," he said, a tremble in his voice.

Lacey stood from the couch and went over to him. She saw the small velvet pouch of the grab bag on the bottom shelf. It was untied and the contents spilled across the shelf.

"What's the matter?" she asked.

"That's not how I left it," Frankie told her.

"What do you mean? It probably just fell out of the trunk and spilled, is all."

"No," Frankie said insistently. "I tied the purse with a knot! A proper one I learned in Scouts. Someone untied it!"

Lacey felt a bolt of shock run through her. Had someone broken into their room and stolen the coin?

She snatched up the pouch and sifted through. But to her relief she found the shimmery gold coin still safely inside.

She held it up to Frankie. "It's still here," she said, with a shrug. "Maybe you made a mistake about the knot."

But Frankie didn't seem placated by the discovery. "I promise you, Auntie Lacey," he said firmly. "Someone had to have untied that knot to get into the purse. Someone has been in here!" He started looking about him, his eyes bulging with terror.

Naomi approached. "What's going on? What are you saying to my son? You've already upset him once today."

"There was a burglar!" Frankie blurted.

"What?!" Naomi screamed, immediately panicking.

Shirley heard the commotion and hurried over. "What's all this fuss about?" she asked.

Naomi grasped her by the arms. "Someone broke into the inn!"

Lacey rubbed her forehead. There was no reasoning with her family when they were in the middle of a collective hysteria. It didn't matter that the coin hadn't been stolen, and that there was no sign of a break-in, and that the far more logical explanation was that Frankie had misplaced confidence in his knot-tying abilities. They'd have to exhaust their panic first before they would listen to reason.

Tom drew up to Lacey's side and wrapped an arm around her shoulder. Together, they watched her relatives run around like headless chickens.

"I'm going to go out on a limb here," Lacey said. "But I'm guessing this wasn't what you thought our Dover getaway would be like when you booked it."

He chuckled. "Which bit? The potential burglar? The crazy screaming man in the restaurant? Or just your family being with us in general?"

Lacey rested her head against him. "All of the above. I'm surprised you haven't run for the hills."

"I wouldn't want to be anywhere else," he said, tenderly.

But Lacey wasn't entirely joking. She'd let her anger get the better of her earlier in the restaurant. Not only had she set a very bad example to Frankie (after her painstaking lesson about doing the right thing) but she'd also shown Tom a side of herself she didn't particularly like. She hadn't handled herself well at all. If someone had broken into their room to steal the coin, she wouldn't be able to say she didn't deserve it. Because wasn't she doing the same thing to Desmond, right now, in a sense, by depriving him of something that was rightfully his? Just because she'd gotten defensive and stubborn.

What on earth must Tom think of her, really, after seeing all that?

Unsurprisingly to Lacey, she struggled to sleep that night. She tossed and turned on her camp bed, her mind constantly replaying the awful argument with Desmond in the Bluebird restaurant. The humiliation was terrible. Lacey was usually a calm person, and she felt bad about how she'd reacted. The irony was she'd always intended on returning the coin to him the next day anyway. But then he'd been so rude she just didn't want to give him a win. It had made her petulant. But she regretted it now.

What if someone did the same to her? She'd have been mortified to discover she'd accidentally sold a very valuable antique! And wasn't it in the antique dealers' code book not to scam one another? She was bringing dishonor onto the whole profession with her behavior. Just because Desmond was rude, that didn't mean she should stoop to his level.

By the time dawn rose, Lacey had made up her mind. She would return the coin after all.

She got out of bed and dressed in the darkness, creeping around quietly so as not to wake any of her slumbering family. She crept as quietly as she could down the first flight of the creaky, wooden spiral staircase into the main room. But to her surprise, her mom and sister were already up, drinking coffee and gazing out the lighthouse windows at the ocean.

"What are you guys doing up so early?" Lacey asked.

"Jet lag," Naomi muttered in her coffee.

"And Leonard the rooster," Shirley added. "What about you? Why are you up so early?"

Lacey twisted her lips. "I've decided to return the coin to Desmond Forsythe. He was right. It's not mine to keep."

Naomi choked on her coffee. "I'm sorry, what did you just say? You're giving a very valuable coin to a horrible man who shouted at you and made my son cry?"

Lacey shook her head. "No. I'm giving *back* a very valuable coin to a horrible man who shouted at me and made your son cry. It's not mine to keep."

"You're crazy!" Naomi cried, abandoning her coffee on the table and leaping to her feet. "You'd make so much money selling it! You could probably retire!"

"I don't want to retire," Lacey told her. She loved her store, her business. Unlike a certain someone, her secret life's goal wasn't to be a kept woman!

"Then do it for Frankie," Shirley interjected.

Lacey hesitated. Trust her mom to pull out the family card. It was a guaranteed way to tug on her heart strings. With that sort of money, she could certainly afford to see Frankie more often, or fly him over to the UK for vacations. She could pay his college fees when the time came. Help him with his first mortgage.

But then she found her resolve. "It's not mine to keep," she said with finality. Then she took her jacket off the hook and slipped it on. "I'll be back for breakfast."

She turned, ignoring her mom's and sister's continued appeals, and raced quickly down the final set of steps. She hurried out the lighthouse before either of them could change her mind.

The farmyard smell was more pungent early in the morning. The chickens were clucking loudly, and Lacey turned to see Helen Ashworth scattering seed for them. She waved to the landlady. Helen paused to watch her, giving her a small nod. Lacey couldn't be sure from this distance, but it seemed as if she'd done so curtly. Maybe Studdleton Bay was like Wilfordshire and the gossip about the fight in the Bluebird Inn had already gotten back to her. Lacey hunkered down in her jacket, wishing the whole altercation last night had never happened. She should've just given Desmond back his coin the moment she'd found it, rather than wasting time getting it appraised and making it even harder to part with.

The sky was growing ever lighter as she followed the pretty tree-lined roads toward the town center. It was still too early for traffic, so the only real noise was the caw-cawing of seagulls above.

When she reached Forsythe's, she noticed the closed sign up in the window. "Dammit," she said.

Obviously it was far too early for him to open his store. Even with the busy summer tourist trade, few business owners chose to forgo sleep just to catch a few early birds.

Lacey decided to take a walk around the block and check out some of the pretty store fronts she'd missed out on seeing yesterday. Perhaps by the time she returned, Desmond would have opened up.

She took a side street, wandering through the smugglers' lanes that her mom, Naomi, and Tom had explored the day before when she and Frankie had been on their own adventure. There were lots of unique and interesting stores, more so even than in Wilfordshire, and Lacey scolded herself for being so hasty yesterday in dismissing the idea of shopping. Still, she'd had a wonderful time with Frankie and that mattered more in the long run.

She passed a bakery that was just opening up for the day, the mouthwatering smell of bread wafting from it. The shutters of the post office next door were rattling open on their hydraulic system. Lacey decided to return to Forsythe's to see if Desmond was also opening his store up for the day.

She turned the corner and walked up to the small store, with its faded green sign and gold writing. But as she got closer, she saw the windows were still dark. There was no sign of anyone inside the store. No lights glowed from inside.

Lacey wasn't sure what to do next. She wanted this whole coin debacle over and done with ASAP so she could forget about it and get back to her vacation. Maybe she should just post the coin through the letterbox? That way Desmond would see it first thing, lying on his welcome mat as he opened up for the day. She could avoid any kind of nasty rerun of yesterday's argument, too.

She bent down to peer through the letterbox. But as she lifted the flap, the door shifted beneath her fingers.

She stepped back, perplexed. It was unlocked.

Lacey peered through the window again, wondering if Desmond had indeed returned during her walk around the block. She couldn't see any lights coming from the back rooms or corridors, but if he'd only just entered perhaps he'd not had time to switch them on.

Lacey gave the door a little shove and it opened further. She pushed it the whole way open.

Inside, everything was quiet and still. The blinds were drawn, making it very dark. The smell of must clung to the air.

"Desmond?" Lacey called.

She took a step inside, disturbing the dust, which swirled up into the beam of light coming from the now open door.

Lacey noticed then that the light was falling onto a red leather armchair, facing the opposite direction. Poking out the top was the wiry hair of Desmond.

"You are here," she said, walking forward. "I came to apologize about the fight yesterday. I was wrong to argue with you like that. You're the rightful owner of the coin."

The man remained silent. She stepped closer.

"Desmond?" she said, reaching for the armchair and spinning it to face her.

Then she recoiled in horror and stepped back, tripping over something on the floor. She scrambled to her feet and hurried out of the store, her mind frantically replaying the image in her mind over and over.

Desmond Forsythe was sitting in his armchair, dead.

CHAPTER THIRTEEN

Lacey stood outside Forsythe's, drumming her fingers on her crossed arms as she paced back and forth. It felt like a million years had passed since she'd called the police, but according to her watch it had been just five minutes.

She glanced furtively at the open door, her stomach turning at the memory of what was inside. Desmond Forsythe had been a curmudgeon of a man, but she'd never wish him dead, and she couldn't help but wonder what had happened to him. A heart attack brought on from his angry outburst at the restaurant? Or something worse? Something like murder?

A sudden flurry of flashing blue lights and wailing sirens came from the end of the street. A moment later, a police cruiser screeched up beside her. The door was flung open and a female detective emerged from the driver's seat. Short-cropped hair framed a long face with sharp cheekbones and a thin, pointed nose. A waist-length black leather jacket completed her look.

"Lacey?" she asked, flashing her badge. "I'm DCI Julie Brass." She spoke efficiently, with a confident swagger. "This is my partner, DCI Sebastian Fryer."

From behind, DCI Brass's partner emerged. He couldn't have made for an odder pairing for the biker-chic detective. He was shorter than her, with the sort of preppy haircut that belonged in the 1950s. He silently scanned the exterior of the store with a hawkish glare. Then, without saying a word, he proceeded in through the open door.

An ambulance had pulled up behind the police cruiser and the crew went right in after DCI Sebastian, though Lacey knew, sadly, that their expertise would be of no use here.

"Can you tell me what happened?" DCI Brass asked.

Lacey turned her attention back to the female detective. "I came to return something," she said, truthfully. "A coin."

"A coin?" DCI Brass repeated, her already sharp gaze narrowing with skepticism.

"A Roman coin," Lacey explained. "It was mixed up in a grab bag that Desmond sold me."

"So you know the deceased personally?"

"Actually, I only just met him. I'm on vacation. But I own an antiques store so I came in hoping to make a new contact."

"And how did that go?" DCI Brass asked. Her tone suggested she knew all too well what kind of a man Desmond Forsythe was.

Lacey shrugged. "Badly, I guess. He accused me of stealing his coin. He was so rude about it, I refused to give it back." She felt her cheeks burn with shame at the memory. "But then my nephew helped me see the error of my ways, and I came back to return it to him."

"And you decided to do that first thing in the morning?" DCI Brass asked.

"It was weighing on me so, yes, I woke up early. I felt awful about keeping it and I wanted to get it out of the way so I could forget all about it and get back to enjoying my vacation. When I got here, I saw the closed sign on the door and went to post it through the letterbox. That's when I discovered the door was open and Desmond was long dead."

DCI Brass raised her brow. "Long dead? What made you think that?"

"The color of his skin," Lacey said. "He was ashen. I know what that means."

DCI Brass paused. "Tell me. Do you see a lot of long dead bodies in your line of work?"

Lacey gulped. She'd put her foot right in it. The last thing she wanted to do was draw attention to her unlucky habit of stumbling upon dead people.

Just then, DCI Fryer popped his head out the door of Forsythe's.

"Dead for hours," he said to his partner. "Looks like it was a single blow to the head."

Lacey winced at the confirmation that Desmond had been murdered. She'd suspected that might have been the case, but hearing it was so much worse.

DCI Brass shot a narrow-eyed glare at her partner. His glance roved over to Lacey, then he shut his lips, as if suddenly noticing the error of his announcement. The subtle gesture was not lost on Lacey. DCI Brass may as well have told him not to speak in front of the prime suspect. The thought made her palms feel quite clammy.

In DCI Fryer's gloved hand, Lacey noticed he was holding something; a bronze candle holder, in the famous French Rococo style. It was the one she'd seen before on the shelf beside the window. She'd recognized the style because Percy Johnson, her Mayfair antiques contact, had a particular fondness for the style, and for candelabras in general; he had many pairs in his collection, lovingly displayed in a locked glass cabinet. Then her gaze fell then to the dull, dried blood staining one of the candelabra's five arms. It was the murder weapon.

Suddenly, Lacey remembered having tripped over something in her haste to get out of the store. It must have been the candle holder, discarded on the floor by Desmond's killer. She'd tripped over the very murder weapon!

Working on instinct, Lacey grabbed her cell phone. As DCI Brass retrieved a pair of blue medical gloves from her jacket pocket and pinged them over her hands, Lacey snapped a picture of the candelabra.

DCI Brass turned her head suspiciously, but Lacey moved her phone behind her back before she noticed what she was doing. The detective maneuvered herself to block Lacey's view, but through the space between the two detectives' bodies she was able to see the exchange of the candle holder.

"Professor Plum in the antiques store with the candlestick," she heard Sebastian Fryer murmur.

As the paramedics exited the store leaving the scene for the police, a taxi pulled up behind the ambulance and a tall man leapt out.

Tom! Lacey realized with relief.

His figure was illuminated by the flashing lights as he hurried toward Lacey. Just as the memory of her tripping on the candlestick had returned to her, she now suddenly recalled having phoned him after the discovery of the dead man, and stammering gibberish like a madwoman. He must've hurried out of the lighthouse inn as soon as she'd mentioned she was at Forsythe's.

He ran over to her, taking her in his arms. Lacey felt a surge of relief run through her.

"What happened?" he asked, the concern in his voice matching the look in his eyes.

Lacey shook her head, too stunned to really speak. "I found him dead. Desmond. Someone killed him."

DCI Brass looked at Tom. "Excuse me, sir, we're in the middle of questioning this witness."

"I'm her partner," Tom said, confidently.

Lacey felt a surge of comfort. Having Tom there was giving her strength.

"Were you together then? Earlier today?" DCI Brass asked.

"Right up until Lacey left to return the coin," Tom said.

Lacey felt reassured. Without any prompting from her whatsoever, he'd corroborated her alibi. It gave her just an extra level of security.

DCI Brass regarded him with caution. Then she took down their details.

"We'll be in touch. Don't leave town, okay?"

Lacey nodded. Where had she heard that before?

CHAPTER FOURTEEN

Lacey poked at her scrambled eggs with a fork. She and Tom had returned to the lighthouse inn after the police station to de-stress. Tom had busied himself in the kitchen making his special turmeric spiced scrambled eggs with sweet roasted cherry tomatoes. It was a dish Lacey would usually devour with relish, but with a murder investigation looming over her, she just couldn't face it.

"Don't play with your food," Shirley scolded from across the breakfast table.

"Sorry," Lacey mumbled.

She gave up on the eggs and switched to coffee. Her trusty companion never let her down, no matter how hollow she felt, or how much anxiety was churning in her stomach. It was a particularly exceptional coffee today, as well, strong and with dark chocolate overtones. Tom had bought a few different bags of organic slow roast beans during his shopping trip with her mom and sister in the old smugglers' lanes. If only Lacey had gone on the trip with them, instead of being so haughty and proud and branching off with Frankie. She'd been trying to prove a point, but all she'd proven was her ability to get into a sticky situation.

"I really don't know how you keep getting caught up in stuff like this, Lacey," Shirley said, as if reading her mind. She was being as tactless as usual.

"It's not Lacey's fault," Naomi replied, in a rare display of sisterly solidarity. She reached across the table and squeezed Lacey's arm. "The universe has a plan for us all. Lacey's is just more icky than the average person's."

"Thank you, I think," Lacey muttered. She was not in the mood for Naomi's Mother Gia act. It was something she'd picked up on a silent beach yoga retreat in her twenties and which still occasionally reared its sanctimonious head.

"I'm sorry, Auntie Lacey," Frankie said. "I feel like this is all my fault."

"Oh darling, no, don't think that," Lacey said hurriedly, forcing a smile onto her face. "You haven't done a single thing wrong whatsoever. This is just grown-up stuff. It'll all blow over soon."

Tom came over to the table with the pot of coffee and topped up everyone's mugs. He finally took a seat. Lacey looked at him, framed by the big lighthouse windows, and smiled sadly. She felt like she'd barely seen him on this trip. From sleeping in separate beds, to spending their days doing different activities, to having their evening meal interrupted by a surly shop owner, they may as well have just stayed in Wilfordshire. At least at home she'd have been able to visit Chester at the vet for her daily therapy sessions!

No sooner had she thought of home than another terrible thought struck Lacey. The police had asked her not to leave town. If they didn't solve this case soon, she'd be stuck here. That meant no work back at the store. No stock trips with Gina. No auctions. No Chester. She'd become some old reclusive spinster stuck at the top of a lighthouse with nothing but chickens for company.

"I, for one, am finding this all rather surreal," Shirley said. "I thought England was supposed to be quaint."

"It's fine, Mom," Naomi said, flippantly. "It's not like England is full of murderous lunatics. I'm sure Desmond's death was just an anomaly. The maritime museum is open today," she said, abruptly changing course. "Shall we go see that boat, Frankie?"

Frankie—whose expression had become a little shocked when his mother mentioned a murderous lunatic—suddenly looked enthused. "Yes!"

Their dismissive attitudes rubbed Lacey the wrong way.

"You guys go without me," Lacey said. "I want a bit of quiet time if that's okay."

"I doubt there's going to be a rave at the maritime museum," Naomi joked, standing up from the table.

"Do you want me to stay with you?" Tom asked Lacey.

Though Lacey very much would have liked Tom to stay with her, she shook her head. "No. I don't think we should let that lot run rampant in town without adult supervision." She nodded at her unruly family, getting themselves ready for the day in their usual chaotic manner.

"All right," Tom said with a smirk. He kissed the crown of her head. "I'll try and wear them out for you," he joked.

"And don't let them eat too much sugar," Lacey added with a forced smile.

She watched them walk away through the big windows of the lighthouse. As soon as they were out of sight, her mind began racing at a mile a minute.

She washed and dressed for the day, then went and sat on the porch step of the lighthouse, letting her thoughts turn over.

The farm was sun-soaked, and the hens were placidly pecking at fresh seed. Leonard the rooster marched over to the hens, flapping his wings with agitation. It reminded her of Desmond Forsythe and the way he'd stormed into the restaurant, arms flailing, clucking his accusations about her stealing the coin.

"How did he even find out about it?" Lacey mused aloud.

The only other person who knew about the existence of the gold coin was Martin Ormsby, the old antiques appraiser. Helen had mentioned he'd worked at Forsythe's in the past, so it wasn't out of the realm of possibility that he knew Desmond. Could he have telephoned Desmond to alert him about the coin being in Lacey's possession? It was certainly plausible. But even if he had, how would Desmond have known she was at the Bluebird Inn restaurant? He'd charged right in with purpose, as if he'd known in advance that was where he'd find her.

And what about the mystery of the untied grab bag and the spilled coins? Had someone really broken into the lighthouse and left without stealing anything? Had they rummaged through the coin bag without noticing the gold one? The extremely shiny gold one that was virtually impossible to miss? Only someone with very bad eyesight would fail to see it.

"Martin..." Lacey murmured aloud, recalling the way the appraiser hadn't noticed the gold coin in the pile of dirty, dull silver ones at first, until Frankie had drawn it to his attention.

Ludicrous, Lacey thought. Martin was too old and frail to break into the inn!

With curiosity, Lacey glanced back through the open lighthouse door at the green door of the apartment downstairs, shut tight as usual. Maybe the other guest made a noise and frightened the would-be burglar away and they fled before they'd found the coin in the pile?

That definitely made more sense.

Although Occam's razor would suggest that Frankie just hadn't tied the grab bag as well as he thought he had, and that it had fallen out of the elephant's trunk and spilled its contents across the shelf. That better explained the lack of anything in the inn being disturbed, the lack of any signs of a break-in, and the fact that the most obvious item to steal—the gold coin—was still lying there.

The sudden ring of her cell phone jerked Lacey out of her thoughts. The chickens scattered, clucking angrily.

Lacey retrieved her cell from her pocket and saw the name of the local police station flashing up on her screen.

That was quick, she thought. They'd barely given her time to digest her breakfast before summoning her for a second chat.

The last thing Lacey wanted to do was get dragged into another investigation, especially while she was on vacation. But she got the distinct impression her hand was about to be forced.

She hit the green button with trepidation.

"Lacey?" came the stern voice on the other end. "This is DCI Brass. We met this morning."

It was a redundant statement; unless Lacey had short-term amnesia, finding a dead body and speaking to a detective was hardly an event someone would forget in a hurry.

"I remember," Lacey replied, calmly. "What can I do for you?"

"We have some follow-up questions to go through," DCI Brass said. "Just standard stuff." She sounded wholly unconvincing. She may as well have just said that they were treating Lacey as a suspect. "Could you come to the station? As soon as possible?"

Lacey took a deep, steadying breath. It was happening again. "I'll be right there."

She put her phone away, resigned to the huge cosmic joke the universe liked to play with her life.

CHAPTER FIFTEEN

Lacey jiggled her knees nervously. Did all UK police questioning rooms look the same? Utilitarian, with that strange sparkly linoleum flooring and white ceiling tiles, and those hard-backed uncomfortable plastic chairs? It was stiflingly hot inside as well, since the day was turning out to be a gloriously warm one. The sort Lacey would much prefer to spend on the beach sunbathing rather than in a police station sweating.

She tugged the collar of her shirt. "Can we open the window?"

From the table across from her, DCI Brass looked up from her paperwork and nodded to DCI Fryer, who had, so far, been completely silent. He stood, looking out of place in his preppy 1950s college boy attire, and pushed open the awning-style window. It barely opened two inches, and did next to nothing to let any fresh air into the room. Lacey wiped her sweaty palms on her jeans.

"Let's go through everything again," DCI Brass said, shuffling her papers. "You're on vacation with your family, right? So where did you travel here from?"

"Wilfordshire," Lacey said. "Devon."

"The UK?" DCI Brass asked, surprised.

"I live here. I moved to England from New York earlier in the year."

"What prompted the move?"

Lacey wriggled uncomfortably in her seat. Her divorce from David was none of DCI Brass's business, and had absolutely no relation to the investigation into Desmond's killing. And yet what choice did she have but to divulge her most painful experience to these probing strangers? Any resistance on her part would look suspicious. Doubly so thanks to the beads of sweat forming on her forehead.

"My marriage fell apart," she said, not quite able to bring herself to say the dreaded "D" word. She was surprised, too, to realize just how much sadness it brought her to admit. She'd barely had five minutes to truly think about the implosion of her fourteen-year marriage. Now she could tell she'd kept herself busy to purposefully avoid thinking about it.

DCI Brass slid her notebook across the table to Lacey. "We'll need your address." She placed a pen on top of the pad.

Whenever Lacey had given personal details to the police in Wilfordshire, they'd typed them straight into a computer system. This seemed like an attempt to get her handwriting, which would suggest there was some piece of evidence from the scene involving handwriting. Lacey filed the thought away in the filing system of her mind dedicated to Desmond's death.

"Something wrong?" DCI Brass commented.

"No, no, not at all." Lacey snatched up the pen and scrawled down the address for Crag Cottage, wondering if she was shooting herself in the foot. DCI Brass would run her address through the system and see she'd had dealings with the police in Wilfordshire on more than one occasion. Any detective worth their salt would follow that up by calling the local police station for the lowdown. If Brass got through to DCI Beth Lewis, Lacey would probably be okay. She and the female detective tended to see eye to eye. But if Superintendent Turner took the call? Well, in that case, she may as well kiss her freedom goodbye.

Lacey slid the pad of paper back to DCI Brass. The detective steepled her hands above it.

"We've received some interesting calls today," she said.

"Oh?" Lacey said.

"Regarding your prior interaction with the victim, Desmond Forsythe. Do you know what I might be referring to?"

"The restaurant..." Lacey said, glumly, her shoulders slumping forward.

There'd been plenty of witnesses to her spat with Desmond, from the serving staff at the Bluebird Inn, to the "Scottish man" Frankie had pointed out at the table over from them, and his female companion.

"Tell me about the restaurant," DCI Brass said, neither confirming nor denying Lacey's hunch.

Her approach reminded Lacey of the school counselor she'd seen after her father disappeared, although there'd been watercolors to paint with and bright cushions back then.

"I was having a meal with my family," Lacey explained. "Desmond came in and accused me of taking something from his store."

"What did he accuse you of taking?" Brass asked.

"An antique coin. A rare Roman one made of gold."

The sound of DCI Fryer's pen scratching against paper as he took notes set Lacey's teeth on edge.

"That sounds a bit more serious than merely taking something from his store," DCI Brass commented.

Lacey knew that there must've been several witness statements indicating that Desmond had accused her of *stealing*. Of *shoplifting*. Of being a *thief*. If DCI Brass didn't hear at least one of those exact words come from Lacey's mouth, it would make her seem like she was trying to minimize the situation.

"He accused me of stealing," Lacey clarified, cringing at the memory, about having the label of thief unfairly attributed to her. "It was all a huge misunderstanding."

"Oh?" DCI Brass prompted.

"I bought a grab bag of coins from Desmond, Roman coins for my nephew, Frankie, that had been dug up from the beach by detectorists. The gold coin was inside the bag. I work in antiques myself, so I knew it was a mistake for that coin to be in there. I was going to return the coin the next day, since Forsythe's was already closed for the day." She swallowed, knowing the next part of the story painted her in a very poor light. "But after Desmond came into the restaurant and accused me of stealing, and made a scene in front of everyone, I guess I got stubborn and refused to give it back." She shook her head, annoyed with her past self for making a poor decision, one that had set her on this new course. Because all anyone who'd witnessed the spat in the restaurant saw—and then relayed to detectives Brass and Fryer—was him accusing her of being a thief and her refusing to return the coin.

"That must've been very embarrassing for you," DCI Brass said.

Not embarrassing enough to kill the man, Lacey thought, but did not say. Instead, she resolved the story with the crucial conclusion. "After I got back to the lighthouse inn and had some time to calm down, I realized I was in the wrong. I returned first thing in the morning to set things right and return the coin to Desmond. That's why I was there so early. That's why I was the first to find him."

But Lacey could tell by the brief exchange of glances between the two detectives that they didn't believe a word she was saying.

"Would you be willing to provide us with a fingerprint sample?" DCI Brass asked.

That was an interesting development, Lacey thought. They must have taken prints from the candlestick they'd found at the scene, the murder weapon. Once they ran her prints against those on the murder weapon, she'd be immediately cleared and this would all be over.

"Sure, that's fine," Lacey said, relieved there'd soon be solid proof she wasn't involved, since her story sounded ropey at best, even to her ears.

"Come with me," DCI Fryer said. It was the first time he'd actually spoken this entire interview.

Lacey stood, realizing her shirt was stuck to her back with sweat. It was extremely uncomfortable, and she wondered if they'd deliberately made the interrogation rooms poorly ventilated to heighten discomfort, or whether it was just another quirk of these old English post-war institutional facilities, along with sparkly linoleum and mint green walls. Either way, the sweating didn't look good for her.

Lacey followed Fryer into the hallway, having a Twilight Zone moment when she saw just how eerily similar it was to the station in Wilfordshire. It had the same boxy wall lights that provided little more than a dull yellow glow, the same fake-wooden plastic doors with small windows at eye height, the same shiny plastic signs above them indicating *Interrogation Room, Evidence Room, Store Cupboard.* It was even in the same font.

Lacey saw the sign above the bathroom door and paused. "Do you mind?" she asked DCI Fryer. A splash of cool water on her face and wrists would be very welcome right now.

DCI Fryer's eyes flickered suspiciously to the female stick figure on the door, then back at Lacey. It was obvious he thought she was up to something.

"You're questioning me as a witness," Lacey reminded him. "Not a suspect. I don't need supervision in the bathroom."

The expression on DCI Fryer's face vanished immediately. "Of course," he said.

Lacey pushed the door open, even more certain than she had been before that the police officers were looking at her as a possible culprit.

The bathroom was at least two degrees cooler than the rest of the station. Instead of just one small window like the one in the questioning room, there were several in a row over the sinks. A cool breeze wafted in with great relief to Lacey.

She approached the sinks and splashed water on her face.

But as she shut off the faucet, she heard the sound of voices coming in through the open window. Curious, she got on tiptoes and peered through the window gap. There was a small paved courtyard with concrete benches and a spindly tree. A few people were smoking cigarettes and chatting. By their clothing—smart office attire—and laminated lanyards around their necks, Lacey deduced they must be administrators at the station.

Just then, one of the internal doors opened and Detective Brass poked her head out into the courtyard.

"Joanne," she called, addressing a woman in a bright pink shirt. "Where are we on that fingerprint identification?"

The woman in pink, Joanne presumably, stubbed her cigarette out under the toe of her sensible office shoes. "I've had confirmation that the pennies arrived at the archaeologist's. I classed them as high priority, since it's a murder case, so we should have the report within ten to twelve hours."

Lacey lowered herself from tiptoes, her mind whirring. Pennies? What did pennies have to do with anything? She'd assumed the fingerprints they'd found were on the candlestick, on the murder weapon. But Joanne had definitely said pennies. And why were they using the specialist services of an archaeologist rather than just the usual forensics? That would only happen if they were handling historical artifacts that required more precise and delicate methods to extract information from

It all came together in Lacey's mind. They *had* found prints at the crime scene, but not on the murder weapon. On antique pennies. Presumably they were pennies just like the ones Lacey had bought in the grab bag.

A harrowing fear struck Lacey. What if Frankie had been right, and his adamance that someone had been in their room at the lighthouse inn was correct after all? What if someone had come in not to steal the coin, but to take something with her fingerprints on it. To frame her.

A loud knocking on the bathroom door made Lacey startle.

"Is everything okay in there?" came the voice of DCI Fryer.

Lacey grabbed a paper towel to dry her face, her heart racing at a mile a minute. She'd made a terrible mistake agreeing to be fingerprinted. But what could she do about it now? She couldn't go back on it, it would look very suspicious.

She headed back out into the corridor, her throat tight with anguish, wondering if she was about to be framed for murder.

CHAPTER SIXTEEN

Despite being small, Studdleton Bay police station had a very state of the art fingerprint machine, unlike Wilfordshire's. Lacey placed her hand inside a big plastic contraption and her prints were scanned with a buzzing red laser. The image of her prints showed up on a screen in shades of purple, like some kind of X-ray scanner at the airport.

"All done," DCI Fryer said.

"How long will it take for the results to come back?" Lacey asked him.

"We're not doing anything with them," DCI Fryer replied. He was a poor liar. "They're just for our records."

Lacey knew better. She was smarter than that. Besides, she'd been through this before.

She raised a skeptical eyebrow. "I know you're running my prints against ones found at the scene. Why else would you be taking them?"

DCI Fryer regarded her calmly, as if weighing up his options. "It'll take ten to twelve hours to process everything," he said, answering her question with as much evasiveness as he could get away with.

That was good enough for Lacey. It confirmed what Joanne had said in the courtyard. The pennies and Desmond's death were linked.

So she had ten to twelve hours to find some solid evidence to clear her name. However, she'd have to get ahead of the police to do it, so she may as well shave a couple of hours off that total right off the bat.

As they headed back through the corridors, Lacey caught sight of a familiar person at the other end of the corridor being escorted toward the reception by a uniformed officer.

"Mom?" she called across the corridor to the woman's back.

Shirley turned. "Lacey? I thought you were staying at the lighthouse for some quiet time."

"I thought you were going to the maritime museum to look at the Bronze Age boat."

"We were," Shirley replied. "But then the cops called us in to answer some questions."

Lacey glared at DCI Fryer. He shifted from one foot to the other, remaining impassive.

"Wait . . ." Lacey said with dawning, turning back to her mom. "What do you mean 'us'? Who else is here?"

But before Shirley had a chance to speak, Lacey's question was answered by three figures appearing through a door opening into the corridor: Tom, Naomi, and Frankie.

Lacey's jaw dropped. She looked accusingly at DCI Fryer. "Even my nephew? He's just a little kid!"

From the other end of the corridor, Frankie put his hands on his hips, pouted, and said, "Hey! I'm eight years old."

At the same time, DCI Fryer simply told her, "We're corroborating statements."

But Lacey knew exactly what they were doing. They'd called her family here to put her story under the microscope. To see if there were any disparities in her version of events and theirs. To see if they were covering for Lacey by providing her with an alibi at the time of the murder. And that must mean she was even more than a suspect than she'd even anticipated. She was their *prime* suspect!

DCI Fryer stopped at the reception door and gestured for her to head out.

"I can go?" Lacey asked, surprised.

DCI Fryer nodded. "Of course you can leave. You weren't expecting us to arrest you, were you?"

So her family had obviously come through for her, then, if she was being allowed to leave. All their stories had synced up.

As they should, Lacey reminded herself. She had nothing to hide.

Lacey followed the rest of her family out into the reception area. DCI Fryer stood at the door watching them quietly.

As they passed through the room, Lacey noticed the pink-shirted woman tapping away at her computer; Joanne, the woman DCI Brass had spoken to about the pennies. If the pennies came back positive for her prints, then it meant they were taken from her room in an attempt to frame her for Desmond's murder. By whom was the real question Lacey needed to answer to clear her name.

Chapter Seventeen

"That was awesome," Frankie exclaimed, as they emerged out of the police station into the bright sunshine. "A real police station! And real officers! So cool."

Since they'd been inside, the day had become unusually bright. Lacey felt dazed, and the brightness only added to her disorientation.

"Where do you want to go for elevenses?" Naomi asked Frankie.

"The tea rooms?" Frankie suggested.

"Good idea," Shirley said. "I'm famished."

Lacey looked at her family and blinked at them all in disbelief. "We were just questioned in relation to a man's death, and you're worried about your appetites?"

"I've gotten used to mid-morning snacking," Naomi said with a shrug. "And yeah, it sucks, sure. For him, though, not us. We have nothing to do with it."

"You don't," Lacey replied. "But they think I do."

Shirley snorted, as if Lacey was obviously talking nonsense. But Lacey knew better. She'd been through this before. She knew what it looked like when the police were homing in on a suspect, and right now, that suspect was her.

"What did you guys tell them?" she asked, anxiously.

"The truth, obviously," Naomi said. She was starting to sound irritated.

"We told them you were with us the night of the murder," Tom assured her. "They asked me if there was any chance you left during the night but I explained how we're all sharing one room and that the floorboards are so creaky there'd be no way you'd be able to leave without waking at least one person up." He chuckled, as if to show how ludicrous an idea it would be.

"Okay, good," Lacey said, nodding, somewhat placated by Tom's reassurances, though not enough to quell the urge to nervously chew her fingernails.

Once the autopsy report was written up for Desmond, it should become clear to the police that Lacey had no window of opportunity to commit the crime.

"And *I* told them you woke up earlier than normal and left before breakfast," Shirley added proudly, as if she was being extremely helpful.

Lacey cringed inwardly. Her mom had inadvertently given the police a sliver of possibility that she was the perpetrator, because she had no alibi for the twilight hours.

Damn! Lacey thought. Why hadn't she just tried the door first of all, rather than wasting all that time walking round the block waiting for Desmond to open the store?

"So?" Naomi prompted. "Can we go on our museum crawl now? I really want to see some old things."

Lacey glared at her. "What?" she asked bluntly.

Naomi shrugged, defensively. "I like museums too! I can be cultured."

That, of course, was not why Lacey was glaring at her sister. She was glaring because of how blasé her sister was being. How startlingly unconcerned she appeared to be. How all her family were. On the one hand, it meant that her family, at the very least, was confident the police would find the real culprit. But Lacey had been through this before. She wasn't naive anymore. She knew how quickly things could be twisted. How the police could become blinkered. She couldn't just leave this in their hands. She'd have to find stronger proof she wasn't involved.

"A man is dead," Lacey said simply. "And you want to just walk around museums looking at 'old things.' The police think I'm something to do with this! Can't you see that?"

"But you're not," Shirley said. "That's obviously absurd."

"Not to them," Lacey countered, flinging her arm behind her at the station building.

Shirley folded her arms. "Lacey, please don't be so dramatic."

Lacey ground her teeth. There was no getting through to them. She took a breath. "Look, you guys go and have fun on your museum crawl. I'm staying in Studdleton Bay."

Shirley gave her a stern look. "Lacey, you're almost forty years old. Are you really going to stamp your foot and refuse to come like a toddler?"

"I *can't* come," Lacey replied in an equally stern voice. "The police told me I'm not allowed to leave town. Half of Dover's museums are technically in the next town over."

Shirley rolled her eyes up to the heavens with exasperation. "Technically. But I'm sure the police didn't mean it like that. They just meant not to drive home. Going to a museum one town over can't be an issue."

"I don't make the rules, Mom," Lacey told her, glumly.

In honesty, Shirley probably was right. Studdleton Bay and the next town over where most of the museums were located were both in Dover. But she was going to use the demarcation in her favor, because she wanted to stay behind and try to untangle the mess she was in.

"Fine," Shirley said with a sigh. "You stay. We'll go."

She looked over at the others, obviously expecting a chorus of agreement. Instead, all she got was a nod from Naomi, a slightly terrified smile from Tom, and a chewed lip from Frankie.

Frankie looked at his mom. "Can I stay with Auntie Lacey?"

"But I thought you really wanted to see some museums," Naomi told him.

"I did," he said. "But that was two days ago."

"Two days," Naomi said with a chuckle. "May as well be a million years ago for an eight-year-old." She ruffled his hair. "Of course you can."

"That's not a good idea," Lacey interjected. There was no way she'd be able to investigate properly with Frankie tagging along; she didn't want to drag him into something dark and dangerous.

Frankie looked hurt. "But I had so much fun hanging out with you yesterday," he said in a sad little voice. "And I never get to see you anymore. Please, Auntie Lacey."

Lacey's heart ached at the sound of his sad little voice. She felt suddenly very guilty for having up and left New York City on such short notice, leaving behind Frankie, whom she adored. The box of Wilfordshire's finest fudge she'd sent him on his eighth birthday seemed like a lackluster substitute for actual face-to-face interaction.

She looked appealingly at Naomi. But her sister just shrugged.

"Okay," Lacey said, caving in. "You can stick with me."

Frankie punched the air with triumph.

She'd just have to find some way of shielding him from the darker realities of her investigation. There must be some parenting trick she could pull out. She'd been a pretty good surrogate parent yesterday, after all. And since she didn't have Chester with her as her sidekick, her nephew seemed like a decent alternative.

But it was the second day in a row she was spending without Tom. She watched him walk off with her mom and sister, with a longing feeling in her chest. But there were more pressing issues to deal with now than the debacle of their disastrous first romantic getaway. Because now there was a murder to solve.

"Looks like it's you and me," she said to Frankie once they were alone.

"Great." He leaned in conspiratorially. "Wanna hear my theory?"

Lacey blinked with surprise. "I'm sorry, what?"

"You're trying to solve the crime, right? That's why you wanted to stay behind?"

So he'd figured out what she was up to. How astute. Maybe having an eight-year-old boy as a sidekick wasn't going to be as much of an encumbrance as she'd originally thought.

"You're right," Lacey confessed.

He grinned. "So? Wanna hear my theory?"

With no other leads to pursue, Frankie's guess was as good as anybody's.

"Hit me," she said.

"What if Desmond stole the coin from one of his antiquing contacts?" Frankie began. "Say . . . a Scottish man with a Highland Terrier and a ginger moustache?"

Lacey raised her brows. Frankie continued, unperturbed by her incredulity.

"So when the man worked out that Desmond had the coin, he went all the way to Forsythe's on the back of his black stallion to demand it back. Desmond was expecting this, so he hid the gold coin in one of those detectorists' grab bags for safekeeping—the one he accidentally sold to you. So when Desmond told the Scottish antiques guy that he didn't have the gold coin anymore, Mr. McGinger Moustache lost his temper, wielded his sword . . ." He mimed raising a sword above his head, Braveheart style. "...and killed him." He brought his mimed sword down with vigor.

Lacey winced. "That's...actually not a bad theory."

"Really?" Frankie asked, a triumphant glint in his eyes.

Obviously the mustachioed Scottish man on the back of a horse with a sword had nothing to do with anything, but the suggestion that someone from antiquing was involved in Desmond's killing was definitely worth further consideration. The antiques world was a small one, made up of a complex web of interconnected cliques. Lacey had discovered as much herself when it turned out Xavier Santino, her Spanish antiques contact, knew her father from his old New York City store. No one who worked in antiquing did so alone. It was impossible to operate in a vacuum. They relied on one another for knowledge and expertise (as she did with Percy), and for support (as with the English Antiques Society who took bus trips to her auctions).

So the idea that Desmond had stirred up some bad blood along the way seemed highly plausible to Lacey, especially considering how unpleasantly he'd behaved during their first meeting. If he could insult Lacey in five seconds flat, how many enemies had he managed to make over the years Forsythe's had been in operation? It didn't take a huge leap of imagination to picture Desmond being the dodgy dealer type either, someone who acted in underhanded ways, who didn't play by the rules of the antique collectors' playbook. The way he'd so rashly accused her of being a thief in the restaurant smacked of "takes one to know one." His choice to do it in the most publicly humiliating manner possible really spoke to what kind of a character he was.

"Let's start by pursuing the theory that this was an inner circle thing," Lacey said to Frankie. "A grudge. A bad deal that caught up with him."

It was as good a place to start as any. Indeed, there was no other place to start at all.

"So we need to find out who Desmond's antiques contacts were," Frankie said. "That's the sort of thing you'd keep on a spreadsheet, right?"

Lacey's mind went straight to her own store's "filing system"—a shoe box filled with scraps of paper.

"Right," she said. "But we won't be able to access Desmond's computer. His store is a crime scene. We won't be allowed inside."

"And I'm guessing breaking in is off the cards?" Frankie said in a hopeful voice.

Lacey put her hands on her hips. "Er, yes, mister. It definitely is!"

Frankie pouted. "Well then, how are we going to find out who Desmond's contacts are?"

It came to Lacey in a flash. "I know! We ask..."

"...Martin Ormsby!" they both cried in unison.

The old appraiser hadn't been particularly forthcoming about whether he had a connection to Desmond during their first meeting, but the two men clearly knew one another in some capacity, beyond the fact they'd both worked at Forsythe's during their careers. Martin was the only other person who knew Lacey was in possession of the gold coin (besides her, Frankie, and the rest of her family, of course), so the chances that he'd been the one to tell Desmond hovered up at ninety-nine percent. It was the only way to explain how the news had gotten back to the surly shop owner so quickly. If anyone knew who Desmond's contacts in the antiques world were, it would be Martin Ormsby.

"But listen," Lacey told Frankie sternly. "We need to be covert. We don't want to make it too obvious that we're trying to solve the case."

"Got it, Sherlock," Frankie said, saluting with flourish.

"Covert, Frankie," she reminded him. "That means no silly nicknames."

Frankie's shoulders sank as his enthusiasm seeped out of him. Lacey felt like she'd just taken a pin and popped the poor boy.

She quickly fetched her notebook from her purse and held it out to him, along with a pen. "Can you write down any names Martin Ormsby mentions?"

From her experience yesterday as designated adult, Lacey had learned that Frankie just needed something to channel his energy into, a role that made him feel important and gave him a reason to focus. But Frankie just looked at the notebook and pen skeptically.

Lacey nudged them closer to him. "Please? I can't be Sherlock without a Doctor Watson."

Frankie grinned. "You bet, Sherlock!" he exclaimed.

He took her pen, then produced his own notebook from his back pocket; the one with the cartoon corgis on it. Lacey smirked.

"Thank you, kind fellow," she said in her best British accent. "But please may I request the young gentleman refer to me from now on as Auntie Lacey?"

"Roger that!" Frankie said, tipping his imaginary flat cap.

Satisfied with her parenting technique, Lacey retraced her route up the hill toward the church, while Frankie pretended to use a magnifying glass.

It was a beautiful day. Birds chirped from the overgrown hedges as they passed.

They stopped when they reached the wrought iron gates of the almshouse. The same little old lady who'd been gardening when they'd last visited Martin was there again. If it weren't for the large sunhat she was now wearing, Lacey might've thought she'd gotten stuck in a Groundhog Day loop.

Lacey pushed open the gate. At the sound of its rusted-metal screech, the little old lady stopped what she was doing and turned. Though her features were obscured by the shadows cast by the wide brim of her hat, Lacey could feel her eyes following them the whole way up Martin Ormsby's path. A prickle went up her spine.

When they reached the front door, Frankie knocked, then stepped back with his hands clasped behind his back in a policeman pose. He gave Lacey a slow, conspiratorial nod.

But as they stood on the stoop waiting for the door to be answered, the prickly sensation racing along Lacey's skin became a thousand times more intense and her ability to play-act with Frankie ceased immediately. She glanced behind at the old woman, still watching them with her shears at her hip. In the archway of the church now stood the vicar, watching them too. And at the exact same moment, a large cloud passed in front of the sun, plunging the entire courtyard into shadows, which was, of course, the perfect time for a crow to start cawing, and a large black cat to streak across the path in front of them. Lacey's spidey senses went haywire, and a sudden, terrifying thought popped into her head.

"Martin could be the murderer," she whispered under her breath.

"What did you say?" Frankie asked. "I didn't hear you."

But it was too late. The front door had begun to open with a slow, ominous creak. There was no time to change course now. Lacey would have to see it through.

The beady eye of Martin Ormsby appeared in the gap. "I was wondering when you'd be back."

Lacey heard the scratchy noise of the chain being unhooked from the inside, then the door was opened fully, beckoning them back inside the dark, dusty house.

Lacey gulped. Was she about to walk into the house of a killer?

CHAPTER EIGHTEEN

Lacey's mind went into overdrive as she perched tensely on the edge of Martin Ormsby's chintzy floral settee. From the kitchen came the clinking sound of crockery as he brewed a fresh pot of tea.

"I hope you like Earl Grey," came his thin, croaky voice from the other room.

"I've never met him," Frankie yelled in reply.

"It's a type of tea," Lacey murmured in a hypnotic voice.

Frankie tipped his head to the side and looked at her quizzically. "Are you okay, Auntie Sherlock? You've gone kinda pale."

It didn't surprise Lacey to learn the color had visibly drained from her face; she'd become quite cold as her thoughts raced through a dozen different gruesome scenarios.

In the first scenario, an innocent Martin went to Forsythe's to inform Desmond about the misplaced gold coin, but in doing so accidentally provoked a rage in the man that culminated in violence. Martin had defended himself with the closest heavy item—the bronze candle holder—and had, against the odds, come out as victor. But Lacey knew perfectly well that in a fight between Desmond and Martin, the latter would come off worse, and so her brain immediately conjured up a whole new scenario, one that better illustrated the facts.

In this new and wholly more sinister scenario, a calculating Martin Ormsby premeditated the whole thing after meeting Lacey and realizing she and the gold coin would provide the perfect cover for his crime. He telephoned Desmond to inform him some appalling American woman had come to him with a gold coin she'd brazenly revealed had been stolen from Forsythe's, thus provoking Desmond into making a terrible public scene at the Bluebird restaurant where there was no short supply of corroborating witnesses. Martin went to Forsythe's after closing, bashed Desmond over the head, doing away once and for all with that awful man, and merrily went back to his almshouse right under the nose of the church and the watchful eye of the nosy biddy in the courtyard. Because who would suspect a sweet little old man when there was an outsider to point the finger of blame at, one who'd already been witnessed in an altercation with the deceased?

Suddenly, the cuckoo clock on the wall began cooing in the hour, and Lacey jumped a mile, her frantic ruminations coming to an abrupt end.

"Gosh, is that really the time?" came Martin's voice suddenly from the door.

Lacey jumped another mile. Any more scares, and she'd've jumped a whole marathon before long.

Martin stood in the doorway holding a silver tray in his hands. The tea set on it rattled as he crossed the room toward them.

"I was all out of English breakfast," he said as he shuffled across the carpet in his slippers. "I hope you don't mind Earl Grey. Some say it's a bit of an acquired taste. A little bitter."

"I guess I won't know until I try," Frankie said.

"What a good attitude you have, young man."

Frankie grinned. Lacey forced a smile, but her facial muscles were as tense as her brain, and it came out as more of a grimace.

Martin set the tray down on the coffee table, making the sound of rattling porcelain echo through the living room. The noise put Lacey even more on edge than she already was. But watching Martin move reminded her just how frail he really was. If a teapot was heavy enough to make him shake, then surely a solid bronze candle holder would be too difficult for him to lift all the way above his head? Maybe her mind had gone into overdrive for no reason. The goosebumps on her arms began to recede.

Martin's shaking continued as he picked up the teapot and poured the Earl Grey into the cups. Steam bellowed up, obscuring his face.

"I heard about Desmond," he said as the mist cleared. "Terrible. Terrible. Dreadful business."

Either he was a well-versed actor or the tremble in his voice conveyed genuine emotion. Lacey didn't know what to think, and she wasn't about to jump to

VEXED ON A VISIT

any conclusions, especially when her gut instinct had been going haywire just a few minutes earlier.

"Biscuit?" he finished, offering up a plate with shortbread.

He was being as polite as ever. Beyond his obvious frailty, surely he was far too sweet to be a killer? Though Lacey had met plenty of people now who seemed nice on the surface but were hiding evil inside of them.

Frankie, oblivious to any of the ruminations Lacey was anxiously stuck in, helped himself to a shortbread.

"Thanks!" he said, taking a big bite and munching noisily.

Martin settled into his armchair. "So what can I do to help you two today? I assume you're here because you have more questions about coin collecting?"

"That's right!" Lacey said, latching on to the idea. "We have questions. Tons of questions."

"Thought as much," Martin said with a chuckle. "Once you get bitten by the coin collecting bug it's hard to shake." He looked at Frankie. "So young man. Fire away. What questions did you want answering?"

Luckily, Frankie had his mouth full of shortbread, which gave Lacey the opportunity to answer before he went off on some unrelated tangent, most likely about Scottish coins.

"We thought you might have a list of contacts you'd be willing to share with us," she said. "People in the antiques trade who you worked with back at Forsythe's, for example."

"Gosh. I'm not sure if I do anymore," Martin said. "I've been retired for twenty years. I doubt any of them are still working, and any contacts I made during my years at the store stayed with it. Mind you, that was a very, very long time ago now."

Frankie gulped down his shortbread. "So there'll be some kind of record at Forsythe's?" he said, giving Lacey a knowing look. "I don't suppose you still have a key to get inside, do you?"

"Frankie!" Lacey said. She'd made it perfectly clear there'd be no breaking or entering! And what happened to covert?

"Goodness, no," Martin said, shaking his head. "Like I said, it was many years ago. I worked for Desmond's father, you see. After he passed, his son Lawrence was set to inherit the place but he decided he didn't want it, so it

111

went to Desmond. Desmond and I failed to see eye to eye, so he terminated my contract."

Lacey's ears pricked up. Martin had just given her a whole other scenario to consider. That Martin had a long-standing grudge against Desmond, one he'd finally managed to settle.

"It was a blessing in disguise," Martin added, immediately thwarting Lacey's suspicions. "I went into appraising and never looked back."

Lacey noticed then that Frankie was writing in his cartoon corgi notebook, trying out various spellings for Lawrence. LORENTS. LAWRENTS. LAW-RINSE? LAWRENCE!

She couldn't help but smile.

"You are eager, aren't you?" Martin said to Frankie. "To be taking notes."

"Well, if I want to have the best coin collection in the world, I have to take it seriously," Frankie told him, lying so effortlessly it made Lacey a little uncomfortable. "I don't want the gold one to be the only rare coin in a collection of duds."

Lacey noticed a shift in Martin then. It almost seemed as if he'd become slightly uncomfortable too.

"We're not keeping the gold one though, are we, Frankie?" she said. "Remember how we decided it wasn't ours to keep?"

Frankie nodded. "Right. It belongs to Forsythe's. Desmond's relatives will inherit it."

"So they can ride the Jacobite Steam Train," Martin added.

"Wait. You heard that?" Lacey asked. The conversation she'd had with Frankie had taken place outside the gates of the almshouse.

"These old protected properties don't allow double-glazed windows," Martin explained, before adding with an awkward tone, "And, well, I'm afraid to say your voices are rather loud."

Lacey blushed. She'd been told that before, by both Gina and Tom, the insinuation being that Americans were less soft-spoken than the English. Lacey had taken offense to that. Her mom, Naomi, and Frankie might have the typical New Yorker voices, but she liked to think the edge had been taken off hers since living in Wilfordshire. Although, she realized now, being with her family had probably made it more pronounced again.

"I guess we know how Desmond found out about the gold coin now," Lacey murmured, feeling embarrassed.

Frankie piped up with a grin. "Yeah! It was my loud voice carrying across the town!"

"I don't think your voice is quite loud enough to be overheard all the way from the lighthouse to Forsythe's," Lacey told him. "Desmond must've found out some other way."

She kept one eye on Martin to see how he reacted to her statement. He continued stirring his tea with a spoon, but something in his eyes told her he'd registered the comment. The little twist in his thin, puckered lips told her he was grappling with some kind of internal dilemma.

"Actually," he finally said, his breathy voice little more than a whispered croak, "I think that was my fault."

Lacey felt her chest hitch. Was this it? Was Martin about to confess to something?

Martin put down the spoon and started using shortbread dunking as a way to avoid eye contact instead.

"Once I overheard what you were discussing, I spoke to the vicar about it," he explained, the dunking becoming more rapid. "I wasn't sure"—dunk—"if I had a Christian duty"—dunk, dunk—"to inform Desmond about the coin." Dunk—dunk—dunk. "Or whether the moral dilemma was yours to resolve."

He dunked the shortbread a final time and the biscuit, now saturated, disintegrated into his tea. He abandoned the cup onto the saucer and finally met Lacey's eye.

"The vicar assured me it sounded as if the dilemma was resolved by your good conscience and I needn't take any further action. But, clearly, the news found its way back to him anyway. I'm ever so sorry. I had no idea Desmond would storm into the restaurant and accuse you like that."

He looked genuinely sorry, but Lacey was too busy reeling through the information to worry about reassuring him.

Martin had told the vicar about the gold coin. But a vicar would be bound by confidentiality, right? He wouldn't tattle. There must've been another link in the chain, someone else who held the key to unlock the whole case.

In the silence that followed, Lacey's ears pricked up to the background sound of clipping shears from the courtyard. Like the ticking cuckoo clock, the clipping sound had been a constant part of the ambience, so easily tuned out. But with everyone quiet, the noise had become suddenly very loud.

Lacey's eyes darted through Martin's net curtains and out to the courtyard, where the little old lady in the sunhat was still busy pruning the bushes. She obviously wasn't the killer—she was older and frailer than even Martin—but, Lacey recalled, she had been there while she and Frankie were having their Jacobite Steam Train conversation! And if Martin had been able to hear them from inside his house, then surely the old woman had been able to from the courtyard.

"Your neighbor likes to garden," Lacey said slyly.

"Doris?" Martin said. "Oh yes, she can't help herself." Then he lowered her voice. "But between you and me, I think she uses gardening as an excuse to soak up all the gossip." He chuckled.

"Is that so . . ." Lacey commented.

She looked over to Frankie and wiggled her eyebrows. By the look on his face, she could tell he already understood what she was attempting to communicate. Dear Doris could be the missing link. They may just be about to crack this case wide open.

Chapter Nineteen

When Lacey and Frankie left Martin's house, Doris was, once more, standing in the courtyard. But she wasn't pruning the bushes anymore, she was busy chatting away with the vicar, who was standing in the doorway of the central church looking (dare Lacey think it) like he wished he could be anywhere else. And "chatting" wasn't the appropriate way to describe it, either. Yelling was more apt.

"Dead!" Doris was exclaiming, waving her shears around. "Dead as a dodo!"

"May his soul rest in peace," the vicar replied.

"Rest in peace my arse," Doris bellowed. "You know as well as I do that Desmond was a dirty swindler who'll be laughed away from the pearly gates!"

The vicar murmured something in a voice Lacey couldn't hear, but by his stance it was obvious he was suggesting Doris lower her voice and not speak ill of the dead.

But Doris continued with her diatribe, unperturbed. "Well, he was! You know what he was like! Preying on the grieving relatives of dead folk! Buying their stuff for a third of the price, then selling it on! Now maybe if he had a little sick child, a Tiny Tim, so to speak, that needed expensive treatment, well that would be one thing. But as far as I know his wife divorced him and there was never a Tiny Tim in the first place!"

Lacey ushered Frankie out of the wrought iron almshouse gates and behind a hedge. They crouched down and she put her finger to her lips.

"What's she talking about?" Frankie whispered, his pen and notebook poised.

"A whole bunch of stuff that might be useful to our investigation," Lacey told him. She tapped the cartoon corgis on the front of his notebook, indicating that he needed to write it down. "She's saying that Desmond didn't have any children. That means he has no next of kin. Which means no one was set to profit from his death. We can strike that off as a motive."

Frankie looked up from his scribbled notes with wide eyes. "Does that mean we get to keep the gold coin?" he asked, completely missing the point.

"I wouldn't count on it," Lacey told him. "People have a way of coming out of the woodwork when money is involved." She tapped the paper. "Add ex-wife to your list. We may be looking at a revenge motive."

As Frankie scribbled his notes, she peered back through a gap in the hedge. The vicar seemed to have finally extracted himself from the conversation with Doris and retreated back into the sanctuary of his church. Doris went back to her pruning.

"Well, we know how Desmond found out about the gold coin now," Lacey said to Frankie. "The whole of Studdleton Bay probably heard Doris yelling about it. Which doesn't really help narrow down our search."

With the whole town now potential culprits, and Desmond confirmed as having no next of kin, Lacey was back to square one. Her prime suspect was a frail old antiques collector who drank Earl Grey tea, ate shortbread, and was so religious he felt guilty over divulging someone else's business to his local vicar. He was about as unlikely a suspect as one could get!

Lacey turned and rested her back against the wrought iron gate, disappointment starting to overcome her. She was no closer to solving this than before she'd come here. The only real thing she'd learned was that if she was in Brass's and Fryer's shoes, she'd make herself the prime suspect too.

"Maybe we should speak to this Lawrence man?" Frankie said, tapping his notes.

"I'd prefer not to hassle the grieving relatives if I can avoid it," Lacey told him, glumly. As much as being under police scrutiny was difficult for her, it was nothing compared to the pain Desmond's family would be feeling. She didn't want to compound that in any way if she could avoid it, even if it did mean taking a longer, harder route to clear her name. Not that they had much time to play with. The results for the fingerprints on the coins would come back soon, and Lacey was pretty confident that they'd frame her for the murder.

"Then what about detectorists?" Frankie suggested. "If the gold coin came from one of them, they're probably the person who wants it back, right?"

"You're right," Lacey said. "But Desmond said there were a hundred of them digging up the countryside." She exhaled. "Face it, Frankie. We've got nothing."

"*Au contraire*, Auntie Sherlock," Frankie said. "We've narrowed down our leads to one hundred!"

Despite her growing sense of hopelessness, Lacey couldn't help but raise a smile at Frankie's unflagging optimism. He was a very good substitute for Chester, who always managed to nudge his nose into her palm at the time when she most needed bolstering. That didn't stop her from missing her poor sick pup, but it did strengthen her resolve to carry on.

"Maybe you were right about going to the store," Lacey said, straightening up to standing and wiping down her jeans. "We might not be able to get inside, but the windows are huge and the killer might have left a clue."

Frankie jumped up and punched the air. "All right! Auntie Sherlock and Watsonbot back in business!"

"Watsonbot?"

"I've decided to be a robot sidekick."

"Of course you have," Lacey said with a chuckle.

They headed away from the almshouse and back down the hill toward town. It wasn't long before Lacey caught sight of the bright police tape cordoning off the front of Forsythe's antiques store, its yellow and blue stripes flapping in the summer breeze.

Flapping? Lacey thought with a frown. *Had it come unstuck?*

As they got closer, Lacey realized the tape hadn't become unstuck at all. It had been purposefully detached at one side and the door was standing ajar.

She caught Frankie by the shoulder and pulled him back behind the wall of the side alley that connected the road to the old smugglers' lanes.

"There's someone in there," she whispered in a hushed tone.

"A detective?" Frankie asked.

"Could be," Lacey told him. "Or it could be the killer."

"Why would it be the killer?" Frankie said, putting his hands on his hips. "They'd be super dumb to come back."

"It's actually very common for killers to return to the scene of the crime," Lacey told him, before immediately reminding herself he was eight years old and really didn't need to know such things.

She peeped her head around the wall, glancing again at the store window. Movement inside made her gasp. Someone was definitely in there, and by their gait and movements, Lacey deduced it was a woman. It could be DCI Brass, only she carried herself with confidence and walked with purpose; yet the figure inside was more tentative, more light-footed.

Lacey squinted through the gloom, trying to pick out any identifying features. It was too dark inside the store to really see. All she could tell was that the person appeared to be searching for something.

Lacey ducked back behind the wall, her heart racing.

"So?" Frankie asked her in a whisper. "Who is it?"

Lacey shook her head. "I can't tell. But I bet they're someone worth speaking to."

Before Lacey had a chance to work out how best to approach the situation, she heard the creak of the door opening, and peered back around the wall in time to see a woman hurrying out. By the look of her skinny black jeans, white sneakers, and off the shoulder T-shirt, Lacey didn't think she looked much like a detective. Of course, neither did DCI Brass, with her biker-chick style, but at least she carried herself with an air of importance. This young woman seemed on edge. Nervy. Jumpy.

Lacey watched as the young woman glanced over both her shoulders, before carefully repositioning the police tape across the door, evidently trying to make it look as though it had not been disturbed. Lacey knew she had to make her move quickly before the woman disappeared off into the maze that was the old smugglers' lanes.

"Stay right here," she said to Frankie.

She stepped around the corner and purposefully bumped right into the woman.

"Ooof!" the woman said, dropping a stack of papers and folders onto the sidewalk.

"I'm so sorry!" Lacey exclaimed.

She crouched down and began collecting up the papers. They appeared to be financial documents.

Lacey looked up at the woman. She was young; nineteen or twenty, Lacey guessed, from the lack of fine lines on her face. Her black wavy hair was styled in an asymmetric bob, chin-length at the front and with a shaved part on one side. A slick of bright red lipstick accentuated her small, pillowy lips.

"Forsythe's?" Lacey read off the top of the pile of papers as she handed them over to the young woman. "Do you work there?"

"Yes," the young woman said, hastily shoving all the pages back into the folder.

They both straightened up. The young woman clutched her folder to her chest. She looked like she was about to bolt, but the invisible social binds of respecting one's elders was gluing her to the place.

"I've never seen you before," Lacey said.

"I'm Desmond's niece, Bernadette."

"Oh really?" Lacey said. "His niece on which side of the family?"

"His brother's," she replied. "Obviously."

"Yes, obviously," Lacey replied with a chuckle, feigning prior knowledge. "Because Desmond doesn't have any relatives on the other side."

It was a guess, but luckily Bernadette fell for it.

"Right. I'm Lawrence's only child. Aunt Natasha died before she and Uncle Desmond had kids."

Natasha? Lacey thought. That must be the ex-wife. And she was dead? She mentally crossed the words *ex-wife* off Frankie's list of suspects. And Lawrence was also on Frankie's list, in several different spelling attempts. This was his daughter. The sole inheritor of Forsythe's. So contrary to what Lacey had heard on the rumor mill, there *was* an heir. And she'd just been found snooping around in the crime scene!

"Sorry, who did you say you were again?" Bernadette said, frowning suddenly.

"I didn't. I'm Lacey. I was a friend of your uncle's." She crossed herself out of respect for the deceased man. "You know, Desmond never did tell me why the store went to him instead of your dad."

"Oh, 'cos after my granddad retired the store was meant to go to my dad, but it went to Desmond instead because my dad already had a career and Desmond . . . well, you know what he was like . . . a bit of a lazy layabout. He needed something to focus on so my dad passed it up and it went to him instead."

"That makes sense," Lacey said. "I guess this is all yours now then? To come and go as you please."

She let her gaze fall to the police tape across the door, trying to give Bernadette a not-so subtle indication that she'd witnessed her leaving the crime scene. She was dropping the bait, to see whether Bernadette would feel compelled to explain her incriminating actions.

It worked. The young woman looked flustered. "Sort of. I mean, not really," she rambled. "I just come here to work during vacations from university, to earn a bit of cash. It's easier to travel here from Canterbury than to go all the way back to Wales where my parents live, and Uncle Desmond needs the help." She looked uncomfortable as she mentioned her deceased uncle by name. "Needed," she corrected herself in a small voice.

Though Lacey knew she should be analyzing Bernadette's words and body language for clues, her mind had homed right in on her mention of Canterbury, the place Xavier had supposedly tracked her father to. Just hearing it set her mind reeling, distracting her from her ability to focus on what the young woman was saying.

"I literally just got the train from Canterbury to here after I heard what happened to Uncle Desmond. My dad called to say I have to meet up with a solicitor. A solicitor! Apparently I'm the sole beneficiary of this place."

"Did you say you go to Canterbury University?" Lacey asked, her mind still stuck on her dad and his supposed link to the city.

"Yeah, that's right," Bernadette said. "It has a great English Literature program. It's the home of the famous Tales, after all." When Lacey remained silent, she added, "Geoffrey Chaucer? The Canterbury Tales? You've heard of it, right?"

"I've heard of it . . ." Lacey said, her voice floating out.

"Did you say you were friends with my uncle?" Bernadette asked. "Where do you know him from? He doesn't have any close friends, and he's never mentioned having an American one. It's the sort of thing I'd expect him to mention." Her eyes narrowed suspiciously, as if it had only just occurred to her that she was divulging information to a complete stranger. "Are you from his fantasy role-playing group?"

Lacey floundered. She was usually quick at thinking on her feet in these situations but the mention of Canterbury had knocked her for six.

"We're coin collectors!" came Frankie's sudden voice.

Lacey turned to see her nephew emerging from his hiding spot. He came bounding over, jumping in to save the day.

"We know your uncle from the coin collecting society," he added.

"The coin collecting society?" Bernadette asked.

"Yup," Frankie said, nodding. "I'm trying to start a coin collection and your uncle said he'd help me."

Bernadette looked curiously at Frankie. "And who are you?"

"Just a local scallywag," he replied with a grin, using the term he'd learned from Arnold the confectioner yesterday.

"He's my nephew," Lacey said, hurriedly, patting his ginger curls. "He has a vivid imagination."

Bernadette looked from Frankie to Lacey. "Right . . ." she said, drawing the word out with suspicion.

Realizing they might be losing her, Lacey quickly refocused her mental energy on the task at hand, putting thoughts of her father out of her mind and fixing a smile on her lips.

"As Frankie said, we're coin collectors. We're on the hunt for an antique coin."

"A gold one," Frankie added.

"A Roman one," Lacey finished.

She watched to see if Bernadette reacted in any way to the mention of the gold coin, but the young woman's face remained impassive.

"Desmond was going to give me a list of detectorists," Frankie continued. "But I guess there's no chance of that now."

He looked mournfully over at the police tape. His acting was a little on the hammy side, Lacey thought, but hopefully Bernadette wouldn't notice.

Bernadette frowned. "You mean the guys with the metal detectors? Why do you want a list?"

"Because they're the ones who find coins on the beach," Frankie said.

"They're always in here selling scraps of metal," Bernadette said, with a shrug, "but I don't know any of them by name. I guess I'll have to learn them now."

She turned her bewildered gaze back to the store, as if the fact she'd just inherited it from her murdered uncle (while in the middle of studying for a degree, no less) was beyond her comprehension.

And while it was obvious to Lacey that Frankie was acting, it was equally obvious that Bernadette was not. The woman was clearly going through a shock. Even so, Lacey couldn't take anything she said at face value. If her uncle had no children, and her father had turned down the opportunity to inherit the store, then Bernadette might well have worked out she was set to inherit his amassed wealth. That put her right in the frame for his murder. And unlike the frail Martin Ormsby, Bernadette was young, healthy, and quite clearly fit enough to strike someone over the head with a solid bronze candlestick.

"Maybe Desmond keeps a list on a spreadsheet?" Frankie offered.

"I mean, I guess I could probably find out for you," Bernadette said reticently. "Uncle Desmond kept records of everything." She peered through the window at the computer surrounded by mess on the desk, a daunted expression on her face. "Although I don't know where to even start." As she turned back, she caught sight of her watch. "Oh crap! Is that the time? I'm running late for the solicitor's! Sorry! Come back later if you still want that list! I don't know how long solicitor's meetings last."

And with that Bernadette hurried away, disappearing into the labyrinthine smugglers' lanes.

Lacey remained gazing at the space she'd last occupied. It was clear enough that Bernadette had no knowledge of the whole debacle over the gold coin. But she certainly had a lot to gain from her uncle's death—more so than anyone else Lacey had met so far—and that meant she was worth further consideration.

Frankie turned to Lacey. "Are we following her or what?" he asked. "See if that whole solicitor story checks out?"

"I think Bernadette has given us more than enough to go on without resorting to stalking," Lacey told him. Then she put her hands on her hips. "And when did you get so good at lying?"

"I'm acting," Frankie said with theatrical flourish. "And I totally saved you! You choked back there."

"Yes," she said, trying her hardest not to get sidetracked by the whole Canterbury thing again. "Credit where credit's due."

Frankie put a hand to his ear. "And . . ." he said.

"And what?"

"And aren't you glad a certain someone suggested we come to the store?" he prompted.

"Of course," Lacey added. She slipped into character. "Thank you, Dr. Watson—"

"—Watsonbot," Frankie corrected.

"Sorry, that's right. Thank you, Watsonbot. What a wonderfully astute suggestion of yours."

But as Lacey turned to leave the scene, her attention was drawn to something displayed near the window of Forsythe's. The large bronze ornate candle holder, in the same Rococo style as the murder weapon. The other one of the pair.

Lacey grabbed her cell phone, remembering the photo she'd taken of the candle holder as it was being passed between detectives Brass and Fryer. She'd meant to send it straight to Percy Johnson to see if he could find out anything interesting about them, but it had slipped her mind. She snapped a photo through the window of the clean, un-bloodied one, capturing its handwritten *three thousand pounds* price tag, then pinged it off to Percy Johnson along with the less clear photo of the murder weapon. If anyone could identify anything useful about the candle holders, it would be him. Of course, she wasn't sure whether that would be useful information or not, but she wouldn't know unless she tried. It could turn out they were part of a rare set and Percy happened to know who they belonged to. It could, more likely, turn out they held no useful information at all, and just happened to be the heaviest item to hand for the killer to strike with.

"What are you doing?" Frankie asked.

She showed him the photo. "I'm sending this to a contact, in case it's a clue."

While Frankie peered at the cell phone with a perplexed look on his face, Lacey suddenly heard the sound of hurried footsteps clattering through the side alley they'd been hiding in earlier, the one through which Bernadette so hurriedly disappeared down. She swirled, on edge, half expecting to see Desmond lumbering along about to give her a piece of his mind again about being a thief, or Martin Ormsby with a bronze candle holder raised above his head in his shaking arms ready to strike. Instead, racing toward her were Tom, Naomi, and Shirley.

"Lacey!" called Tom. "There you are!"

Lacey frowned. What were they running for? And why did they look so animated? So, dare she say, excited?

Frankie started to chuckle. "I've never seen Grandma run before."

"Me neither," Lacey replied, growing more curious by the second.

Finally, the three of them reached Frankie and Lacey, skidding to a halt before them.

"What is it?" Lacey asked, looking from one red face to the next. "What's going on?"

"We were in the maritime museum," Naomi spluttered. "Mom and I were talking." She waved her hand, indicating she didn't have enough breath to continue the story.

Tom took it up. "A man approached Naomi and asked if she was American."

"Our loud voices strike again," Frankie proclaimed.

Lacey frowned with confusion. "I don't get it. You're running because a man asked Naomi if she was American?"

Tom shook his head. "You didn't let me finish! The man asked Naomi if she was American. And *then* he asked her if she was the American woman with the gold coin!"

Immediately, prickles raced all over Lacey's body. She glanced down at Frankie, her surrogate sidekick. His eyes had gone as wide as moons. He was clearly thinking the same thing Lacey was; that this man could be the lead that blew the case wide open! And if this man was important to the case, she didn't want to waste any time tracking him down.

"Did he look like a detectorist?" Frankie asked his mom, miming using a metal detector.

"A what now?" Naomi asked, peering at his admittedly obscure miming act.

"Or more like an antiques dealer?" Frankie continued, adjusting imaginary spectacles in a gesture that was remarkably similar to one Percy Johnson frequently made.

"What is he talking about?" Naomi asked, directing her accusation at Lacey.

"We can explain later," Lacey said hurriedly. "Tell me what happened next. After the man asked you if you were the American woman with the gold coin. What did you tell him?"

Naomi shook her head, looking guilty. "Nothing."

"Well, that's not strictly true," Tom countered.

Lacey's stomach dropped. She didn't like where this was going. She looked from Tom back to her sister and raised an expectant eyebrow. "Naomi? What did you say to him?"

Naomi huffed out a loud sigh. "Okay. Fine. I put on a fake accent and said, 'Gee, I don't know what you're talking 'bout, partner.' Because, you know, I thought it would be funny."

"It was funny, darling," Shirley said cloyingly.

Lacey cringed. Her family still didn't seem to understand how serious this was! A random man asking about an American woman with a gold coin could only mean one thing; that the killer was on her tail. Yet here was Naomi, joking around like she'd just bumped into a celebrity, not a potential thief and killer!

Frankie tugged on Lacey's arm, bringing her back to the issue at hand. "What are we going to do, Auntie Lacey? Should we go and speak to the man? He could be one of the detectorists. Or an antiques valuer. Or someone else entirely. But he must be connected, right? I bet he's really important to our case."

Lacey hesitated. Hearing Frankie refer to it as "our case" was jarring. Her eight-year-old nephew was getting way too involved for comfort. When Chester was her partner she didn't have to worry about him too much; he had teeth and he knew when to use them. But Frankie was a little kid. All he had for protection was Lacey. She'd already exposed him to Desmond Forsythe's fury and taken him to Martin Ormsby's house before realizing the old man could be a killer. She wasn't about to drag him straight into another potentially dubious situation.

She bent down so she was eye level with him. "I think Auntie Sherlock needs to do this one solo."

A frown lined Frankie's forehead. "What do you mean?"

"I mean I'm going to speak to the man alone," Lacey told him.

"But I'm your Watsonbot 5000," he said in a sad, dejected voice.

Though his voice crushed her, Lacey stayed firm. She shook her head. "Not this time. This is definitely an adults only thing. We're not just talking about eating shortbread in Martin Ormsby's living room."

Poor Frankie looked crestfallen. His bottom lip began to tremble. It only strengthened Lacey's resolve, by reminding her he was too vulnerable to be involved.

But Lacey still felt responsible. Frankie had only gotten so involved in the first place because of her. She needed to find a way to let him down gently, so she quickly searched her brain for inspiration.

"But there *is* something you can do for me," she said, hitting on an idea.

"What?" Frankie asked, sounding skeptical.

"You can be my spy. Guard the museum exit. Make sure no one suspicious comes in or out." What she really meant was keep an eye on the family and make sure they didn't do anything stupid, but Frankie didn't need to know that. She held out her hand to him in shaking position. "What do you say? Want to be my double-oh-seven?"

Frankie looked at her hand, stubbornly refusing to take it. But the corners of his lips were twitching upward. Finally, he couldn't resist any more. He grabbed her hand and shook it vigorously. "The name's Bond. Frankie Bond."

Lacey grinned. "That's my boy."

But the comic relief was short-lived. Because now Lacey had to go and confront a potential killer. She turned to Naomi, anxiety burrowing in her gut.

"Tell me everything about this guy."

CHAPTER TWENTY

The maritime museum was enormous, and Lacey felt like a bag of nerves as she climbed the huge stone steps to the entrance. She took one last look behind her at her family, waiting at the bottom of the steps. Frankie was standing with his chin held high and periodically touching his ear, as if receiving communications through an imaginary inner earpiece. She allowed herself a brief smile before returning her focus to the task at hand, clenching her jaw and marching in through the large entryway into the maritime museum.

The cavernous entry hall was full of tourists, crisscrossing the sleek modern tiled floors beneath a huge wooden galley suspended from the ceiling. Their excited chatter echoed around the large space, making Lacey feel very at odds with the happy atmosphere.

Bright sunlight streamed in from the skylights high above her, making Lacey squint as she scanned the crowds looking for a man who matched the description Naomi had given her: stocky, with a navy blue hoodie pulled up over his head, and dirty, scuffed sneakers. Her eyes glossed over carefree children and happy couples until they homed in on a shifty-looking man sitting on one of the concrete benches talking into a cell phone. He matched the vivid picture Naomi had painted for her to a T, and his brooding expression contrasted greatly with everyone else in the museum.

Before embarking on her conversation with a man who might be a killer, Lacey quickly scanned the maritime museum's exits, in case she needed to run. She counted the security guards, as well, placing them on a clock face in her mind. There were three, in her four o'clock, seven o'clock, and eleven o'clock positions. Four o'clock looked like her best bet if any trouble kicked off. He was a young, healthy-looking man, in comparison to a half-asleep elderly man at seven o'clock, and a short, slight woman at eleven.

Swallowing the lump in her throat, Lacey began her cautious approach.

The man was talking into his cell phone. "I'm telling you, it wasn't her. Just some other bunch of Americans."

There was no doubt left in her mind. This was the man she was looking for. Or should she say, the man who was looking for her?

Lacey reached the bench and her shadow stretched over him.

"Hold on," he said into his cell phone, as he looked up at Lacey and glared. "Can I help you?" he asked gruffly.

Lacey summoned all her inner courage. "I think you're looking for me."

At the sound of her accent, a look of recognition registered in the man's eyes. Then they glinted with an emotion Lacey couldn't quite pinpoint, before a Cheshire cat grin spread across his lips.

"I'll call you back," he said into his cell phone, before removing it from under his hood and snapping it shut. "It's you. The American woman with the gold coin."

"That's right," Lacey said.

Here goes nothing.

"Who are you?" Lacey asked. "And why are you looking for me?"

The gruffness she'd seen in the man's face before suddenly softened. He cracked a smile. But there was still something in his expression she couldn't quite read. A disconnect between his smile and his emotions.

He patted the space on the bench beside him. "Why don't you sit down, and I can explain."

Lacey was quietly relieved that Frankie hadn't come with her. The man had a distinctly Scottish accent.

"My name's Angus," he offered when she didn't move. "Angus McRab."

Definitely Scottish, Lacey thought.

"And you already know who I am," Lacey said, coolly.

"Aye. That I do." He patted the bench again.

With her defenses still up, Lacey cautiously lowered herself onto the concrete bench beside him. She perched, poised, alert, and ready to bolt any second.

Angus offered her his hand. She shook it, noting how rough his skin was.

"Why are you looking for me?" she asked.

"My wife and I were spring cleaning," he began, launching into a story that sounded very rehearsed. "I stupidly added the gold coin to a grab bag my wife was donating to Forsythe's, along with a bunch of other low value things. Once she realized what I'd done, well, I was in the doghouse, believe you me."

"I'm not surprised," Lacey said, less than convinced by his story. "A gold coin is hard to mistake for low value."

"How was I supposed to know it was real gold?" Angus said.

Lacey narrowed her eyes, still wholly unconvinced. It sounded like Angus was trying to cultivate a ditzy caricature for himself, even though she'd seen his brooding, surly expression when he'd been on the phone. And even the ditziest of people could recognize gold when they saw it.

"So anyway," Angus continued. "The gold coin is some old family heirloom, and now my wife is devastated. That was her on the phone, crying her little heart out. You see, I tried to get it back from Forsythe's last night but when I got there the store was closed. But the annoying thing is that the shop owner was still inside! I tried pounding on the window but the bastard kept shaking his head, saying it was too late and to come back tomorrow!"

That definitely sounded like the Desmond Forsythe Lacey had met. Stubborn. Unmoved by the plights of others.

"And the most annoying thing," Angus added, "was that the store wasn't even empty! There was a customer inside! While he was standing there telling me I couldn't come inside because the store was shut, there was an old man standing right there!"

"An old man?" Lacey asked, surprised. "Who?"

Angus shrugged. "I don't know. A gray-haired fella. Scruffy type. He was wearing a long green jumper that went all the way down to his thighs."

Lacey stifled her gasp. The man matched Martin Ormsby's description!

"I wasn't going to just leave it," Angus said. "Obviously. So I started pleading through the letterbox, telling him what I told you, about the heirloom and the mistake I'd made, and how my wife was mad about it. You know what he said? He said, 'It's not my problem. An American woman stole it from me. Go and find her.'"

Lacey absorbed Angus's story, trying to place it on a timeline in her mind. His visit to Forsythe's must have happened after the embarrassing restaurant altercation. She wondered if Angus realized he'd just placed himself at the scene of a crime, or if he'd concocted the whole story to cover up the fact he was the perpetrator of it. Maybe his sighting of an old man was made up too, although his description matched Martin too perfectly to have been a lucky guess.

"Did you tell any of this to the police?" Lacey asked.

"The police?" Angus replied. "I don't think the police will be interested in my missing gold coin. I mean they might be interested when I fail to bring it home and my wife chops my head off..."

He didn't know, Lacey realized. He had no idea Desmond was dead.

Or he's playing you for a fool, the voice in her head warned her.

"Didn't you hear?" Lacey said. "The man who runs Forsythe's died."

"Oh," was all Angus said. He looked wholly unmoved. "Well, I can't say that surprises me. He had quite a gut on him, and anyone whose face goes that red when they're angry is probably suffering from hypertension and—"

"—he was murdered," Lacey interrupted.

Immediately, Angus's demeanor changed. He pressed his lips shut. The color drained from his face. It wasn't the sort of reaction one could learn in acting school. Lacey deemed it to be genuine.

"Murdered?" Angus repeated. He looked visibly agitated.

"Yes. And from what you're telling me, it sounds like you and this old man were among the last to see him alive."

Angus puffed his cheeks. "Whoa. That's...that's heavy. Murdered? I should talk to the police, shouldn't I? Tell them what I saw."

Lacey nodded slowly. "It's better to talk to them before they come and talk to you. In my experience anyway."

If she could gently nudge Angus in the direction of Brass and Fryer, that would take at least some of the heat off her for a while.

He snapped his eyes back up to Lacey. "You don't think that old geezer killed him, do you?"

Lacey's immediate instinct was to cover for Martin, the sweet, frail old appraiser. But she held her tongue, because the more Angus spoke freely, the more information he gave her.

"He looked way too old to kill him," Angus added, much to Lacey's relief.

Lacey thought of the candle holder. With the laws of physics on your side, it could become a deadly weapon in anyone's hands. Anyone with the arm strength to lift it over their head, that is. Something made of bronze would be heavy. But too heavy for Martin? That was the real question.

"Man, it's a good thing I bumped into you," Angus said. "Or my wife would literally have killed me when I got home. Accidentally getting caught up in a murder case *and* coming home without her gold coin ..." He shook his head and whistled. "Even the doghouse would've been too good for me." He chuckled and held his hand out to Lacey, his palm up. "So, can I have it?"

She frowned. "I'm sorry, what?"

"The gold coin," he said, his hand still out. "Can I have it back?"

"The coin?" she said, understandably hesitant. Angus had just admitted to being at the location of a crime. He'd offered zero proof the gold coin was really his, beyond knowing it was in a grab bag, something he could easily have heard on the grapevine, since Doris had clearly been loudly gossiping about it while in the almshouse's courtyard. Really, there were infinite routes of gossip he could have found out about the gold coin through. She wasn't just going to take his word for it.

"Well?" Angus said, impatiently.

"I don't carry it around in my pocket," Lacey told him. "And even if I did have it on hand, I'd need to see some kind of proof it was yours before I gave it to you."

"You what?" Angus said gruffly. The stern frown was back on his face.

"Antiquing is my profession," Lacey explained, keeping her voice calm to counter the rising tension. "I'd prefer to handle it properly and carefully. If it's already been lost once, all the more reason to approach it in an organized way."

Angus suddenly rose from the stone bench and loomed over her. He was a tall man, taller than Tom, who was over six foot, but with his width it made him appear even larger than life. His glower and stance made him appear even more threatening. "What are you talking about, lass?"

Lacey stood up, too, and took a step away from him to try and gain some distance. But Angus just stepped forward, closing it again.

"I'm sorry," she stammered. "But I don't want to just hand over something valuable to you. We'll need solicitors ..."

"Solicitors?!" Angus bellowed.

His voice had risen loud enough now to draw the attention of the museum-goers. For the second time in as many days, Lacey found herself becoming embroiled in a public altercation. The way Angus had curled his hands into fists was not lost on her.

"I don't know what kind of circles you move in, love," he continued. "But I'm not the type of guy who has a solicitor!"

"Then a mediator will do," Lacey said, trying to keep her voice even. "I have contacts in the antiquing world..."

She reached for her cell phone in her pocket, as if to find a contact, when in reality she wanted to quick dial Tom. Angus's batted her hand away before she had the chance.

Lacey gasped from the physical contact. Her heart started to race. This had gotten very heated very quickly. And the fact Angus was so quick to temper, on the verge of physical violence over a small dispute, made it seem far more plausible he'd done the same with Desmond Forsythe.

Was Lacey squaring off to a killer?

Just then, a loud woman's voice exclaimed, "Hey!" It carried across the atrium, clearly directed at them.

Lacey allowed her gaze to dart over her shoulder, expecting to see the female security guard leaving her eleven o'clock position and hurtling over. That wasn't what she saw at all. She had to do a double take to really accept it. The voice belonged to her mom, who was running toward them brandishing one of her boating shoes, with a look of fury on her face.

Immediately, Angus took a step back from Lacey. The boating shoe came arcing through the air at him like a missile. It hit the ground, only narrowly missing him.

"This isn't over," Angus sneered, before slinking back and getting lost in the crowds.

"What is this lunatic doing?" Shirley was yelling shrilly. "He's threatening my daughter! Where are the guards? Who runs this place? Guards!"

She was starting to cause a scene. People turned to watch the unfolding drama, whispers passing between them. Lacey started seeing cell phones pop up as a few crass onlookers captured what they clearly hoped would be the next viral internet moment.

Shirley reached Lacey, grabbed her by the shoulders, and pulled her into a bone-crushing hug. "My baby!" she wailed. "What was that horrible man saying to you?"

Lacey wasn't sure whether to feel embarrassed or relieved. In a matter of moments, she'd gone from being threatened to being protectively held—albeit by a woman who was only wearing one shoe and panicking so loudly she'd drawn in quite the crowd.

"Nothing, Mom. Nothing. It's fine," she finally said.

But as she said it, she could feel herself begin to tremble. The whole thing had rattled her. At the smallest of provocations, Angus McRab had shown his true colors. Was it possible he'd gotten angry enough to kill Desmond Forsythe?

CHAPTER TWENTY ONE

"You know, Mom, that was kind of amazing," Lacey said to Shirley once she'd recovered enough to get her breath back. It wasn't often that her mom had her back like that. She was still in telephone contact with Lacey's ex-husband, for goodness' sake!

"No one messes with my baby," Shirley told her fiercely.

Just then, the sound of footsteps clattered across the museum's atrium toward Lacey. Suddenly, she found herself standing right in the center of the security guards, her family, and a small crowd of onlookers. She wasn't sure what was worse: being threatened by Angus or now being the center of everyone's attention. She squirmed, uncomfortable to have so many pairs of eyes on her.

"Is everything okay, miss?" the four o'clock museum guard asked her.

"That guy was accosting her!" Shirley exclaimed, pointing into the crowds Angus had disappeared into.

"Can you give us a description?" the eleven o'clock guard asked, her voice as thin as her frame.

There was a flurry of motion to one side as someone barged their way through the crowd. Tom! Naomi and Frankie were hot on his heels.

Tom raced up to Lacey and scooped her into his arms. "Lacey, what happened? Are you okay?" The concern in his voice was palpable.

Lacey buried her face into his chest, breathing in his comforting scent. "It's nothing," she murmured, feeling secure in his arms. "I'm fine now."

She didn't want to talk about the altercation here in front of everyone, and especially in front of Frankie. She felt terrible for dragging him into so much drama. Not that he looked scared—he actually looked rather excited by it all— but that didn't make it okay in her mind.

"That big man was shouting at her!" someone in the gathered crowd blurted.

"And then that woman threw her shoe at him!" a kid cried.

Naomi's eyes widened as she took in the sight of Shirley's stray shoe, and her shoeless foot, before burying her face in her hands with embarrassment. But Tom's reaction was quite the opposite.

The change in Tom was instantaneous. He went from being protective to being riled.

"What man?" he demanded, looking around furiously. "Who is he? Where did he go?"

"Tom, please," Lacey said, trying to calm him down. "The last thing I need is for you to get into a macho-man contest with an angry Scot."

"A Scot?" Frankie exclaimed. "Was he Scottish?"

Lacey rubbed her forehead. What a silly slip-up for her to have made in front of Frankie!

"Are we still talking about coin man?" Naomi asked, looking confused. "He was Scottish? Well, I guess he did have a weird accent, now I come to think of it."

"Do you want us to telephone the police, miss?" the elderly guard asked Lacey.

She shook her head. It was starting to pound. "No, that's not necessary."

"Wow! A real Sottish man!" Frankie sang, dancing on the spot.

A hubbub was rippling through the crowds. All the voices clamoring over one another was starting to make Lacey's vision spin. All the eyes were making her feel scrutinized.

"Everyone. Please. Shut up!" Lacey finally cried.

Silence fell. An awkward, uncomfortable, hushed silence. Lacey's insides squirmed at the stunned look on her loved ones' faces. They'd never seen Lacey put her foot down quite so forcibly before.

"I don't want to call the police," she told the guards, calmly. Then to her family, she said, "I'd just like to get out of here, please. I'll tell you everything once I've had a stiff drink."

"A drink?" Naomi said incredulously. "It's a bit early for booze!"

"Since when were you the sensible one?" Lacey replied.

Naomi held her hands up in truce position, and, for once, Lacey's family actually listened to her. They headed for the exit.

As they crossed the large atrium of the museum, Lacey felt as if every pair of eyes was following her. She stuffed her hands into her pockets, hunkering down to avoid their judgmental gazes.

They filed out the doors and down the steps onto the busy pavement below.

"Where do you want to go?" Tom asked Lacey. He used a careful tone, like she was some kind of invalid. Lacey didn't like to be made to feel helpless.

"There," she said, pointing at the roughest-looking pub she could see, a real Tudor building complete with a timber frame and small, smudgy glass windows.

The sign hanging above it said *The Cavern* and showed a picture of an ugly pirate holding up a tankard of ale. Yes, that seemed like a perfectly appropriate place to hide to Lacey.

They headed inside.

It was dark, hot, and stuffy in the pub. The ceiling was so low, Tom could barely stand up fully, and he had to duck so as not to hit his head on the wooden beams. The wooden floorboards sloped downward, and the walls bulged inward, giving Lacey a sense of claustrophobia. Instead of tables, there were stools set around wooden wine barrels. Every last inch of wall was decorated with pirate memorabilia.

"This was the smugglers' bar!" Frankie squealed with delight.

"Don't go getting any ideas," Naomi warned him.

The bar itself was set back into a sort of nook. On a chalkboard on the wall, all the different types of rum were listed in cursive white chalk. A cartoon pirate with a blackened front tooth grinned at the bottom.

"I've never been in a place like this," Shirley commented. She looked out of place in the dingy surroundings, but the smile on her face made it clear she was having the time of her life.

"Tom, you should pick the drinks," Naomi suggested. "You're the foodie, after all."

"I've found us a table!" Frankie called.

He was sitting in a wooden booth shaped like a crow's nest, with netting and rope hanging around it like that from a ship. A candle in a wine bottle burned on the table, its wax having dripped onto the surface of the table. To Lacey's surprise, her mom and sister seemed to think it was quirky, rather than unhygienic as she would've expected.

As Lacey slid into the booth, she heard her phone ping with an incoming message. She checked and saw it was Percy Johnson replying to her inquiry about the candle holder.

Yes, those are 5-armed bronze Rococo candelabras. They're quite common, and the ones in the photos aren't the best condition I've ever seen. A pair in pristine condition can fetch up to £3,000, as the label has it listed at, but with all those scuffs and scratches, I'd value that one at £800. And of course, if there's just one, it would fetch even less. Most people want their candle holders in pairs.

Lacey pondered the message. So Desmond had priced the candle holder at over three times its actual price? Either he was completely mistaken as to the condition of the candle holder and assumed it could fetch the higher price, or he was just trying his luck. Lacey couldn't be certain. But from what she'd learned from Doris, Martin, and Bernadette, the latter was more likely than the former.

Desmond was a swindler. Had his reputation caught up with him?

Tom came over to the table and placed down an array of colored cocktails.

"A daiquiri for Shirley," he said, placing the classiest-looking glass in front of her. "Naomi, I figured you were a mojito kind of girl."

"You guessed right," Naomi said, grinning devilishly.

"And for you, Lacey, a Long Island iced tea. I thought you might appreciate a taste of home." Then under his breath, he added, "There's four shots in that thing. Go easy."

Lacey took a sip of her drink. It tasted exactly how she was expecting, like an iced tea, only with a cola overtone and orange juice squeezed in for good measure. It was exactly what her frayed mind had been hankering for; something delicious and exceptionally boozy. She felt the tension in her muscles immediately begin to melt away.

Tom took his seat opposite her. He always looked exceptionally handsome in the candlelight, with the yellow light accentuating his sharp jawline, but now he looked even more gorgeous than ever. Perhaps it was because they'd not had much time together recently. Or perhaps it was the glass of Dark and Stormy in his hand, which gave him a suaveness he was usually too goofy for. Or maybe it was the effects of her vodka, gin, rum, tequila, triple sec combo! Lacey hurriedly put her glass back down, reminding herself to pace.

"You've got your drink," Tom said. "Now it's time to tell me what really happened back at the museum."

Lacey flicked her gaze over to Frankie. She'd prefer not to discuss this stuff in front of him.

"Oh, he's fine," Naomi said, noticing where Lacey's gaze had gone and waving her concerns away in one fell swoop. "He's watched *Braveheart* about a million times."

Letting an eight-year-old watch *Braveheart* was questionable in itself, but Lacey wasn't about to challenge Naomi's parenting decisions. She began to explain what had happened.

"His name was Angus," she said. "And he claimed to be the original owner of the gold coin. He wanted it back but I obviously wasn't going to just agree to that without any proof it was actually his in the first place. He didn't take too kindly to that."

She took a swig of her cocktail as the scary moment replayed in her mind's eyes.

"How else would he have heard about the gold coin, though?" Tom asked. "If it wasn't his."

"Studdleton Bay's like Wilfordshire," Lacey told him. "There's a gossip train." She pictured Doris with her sunhat and shears. "Believe me, news gets around."

"Do you think Angus killed Desmond?" Frankie asked.

"I don't know," Lacey said. "He seemed genuinely shocked when I told him Desmond was dead. But that could've just been an act." She took another deep sip of her Long Island iced tea, feeling it warm her insides. "The thing is, he admitted to having gone to Forsythe's the night of the murder. He said he saw Desmond inside talking to someone."

Naomi snapped her fingers. "Well, there you go. That's obviously the guy, right? Case closed."

"But he might've just been saying that to throw Lacey off the scent," Tom countered.

"Why would he risk putting himself at the scene of the crime if he hadn't actually seen something?" Naomi rebuffed.

"To send Lacey on a wild goose chase," Shirley offered.

"Did he describe the man who was at Forsythe's?" Tom asked. "Is there any way we might be able to track him down?"

Lacey twisted her lips. "That's the thing. The man he described sounded exactly like Martin Ormsby."

"The appraiser?" Frankie gasped. He looked crestfallen. He'd obviously taken quite a shine to Martin Ormsby.

Naomi looked appalled. "The guy you two visited?" she asked. "Lacey? Did you take my kid to a murderer's house? Did you let my kid eat a murderer's shortbread!"

"I'm not a kid," Frankie said, at the same time that Lacey shushed her sister. Naomi was talking loud enough to draw the attention of the other customers sitting nearby, and Lacey had quite enough of being the center of attention for one day.

"I don't think Martin's the killer," Lacey continued. "He's very old, and quite frail. I mean, he was shaking just holding the teapot, for goodness' sake. I can't imagine him having the strength to ..." She stopped, overtly aware of how Frankie was leaning in to get more of the gruesome details. "You know. Besides, he doesn't have much of a motive. He worked with Desmond at Forsythe's briefly twenty-odd years ago, then left the job to become an appraiser. If he had some kind of grudge or score to settle, he certainly took a very long time to do it."

"Which makes Angus look like a more likely suspect again," Tom offered. "He could've gone to the store to steal the gold coin, only realizing after Desmond was ... you know ..." He paused, side-eyeing Frankie, before whispering, "... D.E.A.D ... that it wasn't at the store at all."

"Conjecture," Frankie said.

Tom raised an eyebrow. "Huh?"

"It means," Frankie said, tapping his cartoon corgi notepad, "that you're forming an opinion without enough information."

"He's right," Lacey concurred. "All we know about Angus is that he knows about the gold coin and has a quick temper."

"And that he's Scottish," Frankie added, as if it was of any importance at all.

"Him being from Scotland isn't really anything to do with it," Lacey said. But then she paused to reconsider. Maybe Angus being from Scotland was relevant after all? It meant he wasn't born and raised in Studdleton Bay. He'd either moved here from Scotland at some point, when he was old enough for his accent to be fixed, or he didn't live in Studdleton Bay at all. If he was just a visitor, then his story about donating the grab bag during a spring clean would fall apart. It would also make it unlikely that he knew Desmond personally. Most killers knew their victims. But if Angus was from out of town, why had he traveled to Studdleton Bay of all places to commit his crimes?

"Victims are usually known by the perpetrator, right?" Tom said, as if reading her thoughts.

"Right."

"So Desmond's family might be a good place to start."

Frankie became animated. "Ooh! I know about this. Desmond has a brother named Lawrence, a niece named Bernadette, and an ex-wife named..." He trailed off and looked at Lacey.

"Natasha," she told him, filling in the blank. "But she's deceased."

"She is?" Frankie said.

"Sorry, I forgot to tell you. You can cross her off the list."

Naomi's frown deepened. "Why is Frankie in charge of your suspect list?" she asked.

"I'm Watsonbot," Frankie said, without looking up from his very important note-keeping task.

Naomi glared at Lacey next.

"He wanted to help," Lacey said, feeling insecure. So much for Naomi's questionable parenting decisions. She'd been the one to irresponsibly involve her nephew in this whole case. Who encouraged him to play Dr. Watson and James Bond. To lie. A somber mood fell over her as she realized she didn't have this parenting thing down quite as well as she thought she did.

The rest of the occupants at the table seemed just as morose. It was a heavy situation, and they all seemed to be feeling the strain.

"We need to speak to Martin again," Frankie said, looking up from his notebook and breaking the silence.

"What?" Naomi exclaimed incredulously. "No way! You're not going to that shortbread eating, Earl Gray drinking murderer's house ever again!"

"But we could ask him if he went to Forsythe's the night Desmond died," Frankie explained. "If Martin admits he was there, then Angus was telling the truth about seeing him there, and we'll know he really is the owner of the gold coin."

Everyone regarded him.

"He's a smart one," Tom said with a nod.

Frankie let out a proud smile. But Lacey was less enthused. The clock was ticking for her. It wouldn't be long before the cops got the fingerprint results back on the pennies, and she was pretty sure they'd be a match for hers, since the pennies were likely taken from the lighthouse inn to frame her. She didn't have any time to waste.

She stood.

"Where are you going?" Shirley asked, looking from her half-finished drink back up to her.

"You finish your drinks," Lacey said. "I have something to do."

"Can I —" Frankie began.

But Lacey cut him off. This time she was going alone. "Stay with these guys. Take as many notes as you can. Keep your eyes peeled for clues."

"Aren't you coming back?" Tom asked. He looked just as hurt as Frankie at her sudden departure.

"I don't know," Lacey said. "Maybe. Probably not. I'll see you guys later." Then, as her mind went to the police officers, she added, "Hopefully."

Then she hurried away before anyone else at the table had a chance to manipulate her into staying with their sad, puppy dog eyes. Especially Frankie. She'd involved him far too much for comfort. She was going to have to finish this without a sidekick. No Chester. No Frankie. This time, she was going it alone.

CHAPTER TWENTY TWO

Lacey hurried up the hill toward the church for the third time during her short vacation. She could hear the *clip clip clip* of Doris's shears before the almshouse gate was even in view. Surely there'd be no hedges left soon!

She pushed open the wrought iron gate. Its creak caused Doris to turn. As before, the little old lady stopped what she was doing and watched Lacey as she headed toward Martin's front door.

"He's not there," Doris called out.

Lacey paused and then turned. The woman was standing with her shears at her hip. There was no sun hat to hide her features today, and her suspicion was written all over her face.

"I'm sorry?" Lacey asked.

"Martin," Doris's loud voice continued. "He's gone out. Are you family? I keep seeing you round here."

Lacey wasn't sure how much she should divulge to Doris. She felt bad to admit it, but the woman gave off weird vibes that made Lacey's neck hairs stand on end.

"I'm visiting him for work," Lacey said, bending the truth slightly. "We're both in the antiques trade."

"Oh, I see," Doris said with a suspicious look in her eyes.

"Do you know where he went?" Lacey asked.

"Probably to Ashworth's Farm to buy up his eggs for the week. A creature of routine, is our Martin Ormsby. He likes eggs for breakfast three times a week. Helen's chooks make the tastiest ones, in his opinion. I wouldn't buy anything off Helen myself. Horrible woman."

Lacey tried to make sense of the barrage of information Doris had given her. Firstly, that Martin had a connection to the very farm he knew she was staying at, even though he'd failed to mention that once during their visits. It had come up in conversation that her family was staying in the lighthouse inn, so why had he not said anything?

The second was that Doris thought Helen was a horrible woman.

"Do you mind me asking why you dislike Helen?" Lacey asked.

Doris was more than happy to oblige. "She bought the lighthouse after Jimmy Swann died and turned it into a B&B of all things! Swindled his family out of a bunch of money too. She and that horrible dead fellow."

Lacey blinked, perplexed. "I'm sorry. What do you mean?"

"Desmond, that guy who got murdered, he made his money from buying the contents of old folks' estates off their grieving relatives. Does it as a job lot because a lot of people just want it over and done with, and they're too over-whelmed to sift through their loved ones lifetime's worth of stuff. Desmond likes to pretend he's doing a good deed, but he only does it so he can get hold of hidden gems and antiques off the old folk. He says he's an antiquer, but he's more like a pawn broker. A swindler. Taking from the needy and profiting from it."

Doris spoke so fast, Lacey's mind spun. The old woman was an untapped source of information, with a very loose tongue and no qualms about airing others' dirty laundry.

"And Helen!" Doris continued. "She knew well enough what Desmond was up to, but she wanted to buy the lighthouse quickly and so she recommended Desmond's services to Jimmy's family after he died. They lost out on a lot of money because of her!"

"When did this all happen?" Lacey asked, tapping into the goldmine.

But before Doris had a chance to answer, the vicar appeared in the archway of the church. He gave her a stern look, as if warning her not to say another word. At the same time as Lacey witnessed the curious, silent communication between the two of them, the almshouse gate squeaked open and a man entered. He looked somewhat out of shape, and as if the walk up the hill to the church had taken great effort. There were large sweat patches staining the armpits of his white shirt, and beads of sweat dripping down his face. He wore a very troubled look as he hurried past the two women toward the church.

The vicar had clearly been expecting him. He gestured into the church and the man scurried inside. But before the vicar himself turned, he gave a parting warning look to Doris.

Doris went right back to her pruning, her lips well and truly buttoned. As much as Lacey assumed the vicar's warning glare was a reminder to Doris not to gossip or speak ill of the dead, she couldn't help but wonder if there'd been more to it.

Whatever it was, there'd be no more gossip to glean from her. The gold mine had been shut down.

At least Doris had given Lacey some interesting information to follow up. And she knew exactly where to start: the lighthouse. She wanted to see if Martin was indeed at Helen Ashworth's organic farm produce store, and if so, why he'd chosen to omit that bit of information when they'd first met. She distinctly recalled Frankie mentioning the inn they were staying at, and Martin saying he didn't know it. In fact, it was one of the first conversations they'd shared in his antiques-filled kitchen when she'd been delighting in making tea with all his vintage items.

She began her journey back to the inn, feeling somewhat bitter that during her so-called vacation she'd barely seen anything of the town and had been using it as nothing more than a thoroughfare between the lighthouse and almshouse. If there was any good to be found in that, it was that she'd most certainly been getting in her daily exercise. And she'd probably get a pretty nice tan out of it, too.

As Lacey crisscrossed from one side of the town to the other, she felt her phone vibrate with an incoming message. It was from Gina.

Immediately thinking of Chester, Lacey opened it. Her screen filled with the sweet, soppy face of her dog, and Gina's accompanying text saying, "Our daily cuddles. Chester misses you! Hope you're having the most relaxing vacation ever!"

Relaxing, Lacey thought wryly. She barely knew the meaning of the word!

Still, it was a good reminder that no matter how stressful things were for her right now, Chester was having it far worse. Because he was stuck in a strange kennel, feeling unwell and completely unable to understand what was happening to him and why he'd been abandoned.

Seeing Chester made Lacey's heart ache. She'd been distracted enough with Frankie before to have been able to put him out of her mind. But now she was going solo, she really felt his absence. What she wouldn't give to have him by her side, looking up at her with his perceptive expressions, barking his opinions.

He wouldn't have let Angus McRab get so close to her either, Lacey knew that for certain.

Just then, the tip of the lighthouse appeared in Lacey's eyeline. She quickened her stride, eager to reach the farm and see whether Martin was anywhere to be found. She wanted to know if Angus's story was true, whether Martin had indeed been to Forsythe's the night of Desmond's death.

She reached the gates, gazing across the dusty farmyard at the red-painted barn. She could just make out the figure of Helen through the large open doors. She was stacking shelves with her jars of homemade preserves. There didn't appear to be any customers inside, let alone Martin.

Lacey drew closer. The calico cat was sunning itself outside and let out a sweet meow. The noise caused Helen to turn sharply toward the open barn doors.

"Lacey!" she exclaimed, putting a hand to her chest as she crossed the barn toward her. "You frightened me."

"I did?" Lacey asked, surprised. She was a guest at the lighthouse inn, for goodness' sake. Surely Helen was expecting to bump into her on occasion. Why so jumpy?

Unless . . . news of Lacey's altercations with both Desmond and Angus had gotten back to her. Perhaps she was suspicious of Lacey now, of this woman who'd instigated not one but two public spats in as many days. That would certainly explain her being so on edge.

"I wanted to try some of your famous eggs," Lacey said, casually. "I've heard on the grapevine they're the best in Dover."

"Right, yes, of course," Helen said, sounding flustered. "I'll fetch you a carton."

"Oh good, I'm glad you still have some in stock," Lacey said, slyly. "I imagine they sell out rather quickly. First thing in the morning."

Helen wasn't taking the bait. But as she filled up a carton with eggs from the little straw-filled display box, Lacey noticed her eyes flicking over her shoulder at the barn door. Some instinct inside Lacey told her she was up to something.

She paced over to the barn doors—ignoring Helen's cry of "Don't forget your eggs!"—and poked her head out. And there, Lacey discovered, coming out of the door of the lighthouse inn, was none other than Martin Ormsby.

Martin Ormsby was her thief!

Chapter Twenty Three

"What are you doing?" Lacey demanded as she marched across the dusty farm ground toward Martin, making chickens scatter every which way.

At the sight of her, the old man's face turned quite red. Lacey scanned him, trying to see if he had anything of hers on him, something else to plant at the scene of a murder to frame her.

"Lacey, I was just coming to see you," he said.

Lacey shook her head. "Oh no, no no. Don't try worming your way out of this. I saw you coming out of the lighthouse! How did you get inside? Did Helen give you the key?"

She glanced behind just in time to see Helen duck back from the open barn doors. She was snooping again, just as she had the day before.

"The front door was already open," Martin said. "I think the guest beneath you must have forgotten to lock it."

"So you figured you'd just march right on in?" Lacey said, narrowing her eyes. She wasn't buying Martin's explanation one bit. He'd entered the lighthouse to find something to frame her with. "What did you take?" she demanded. "The coin? Did you come for the coin?"

"I didn't take anything!" Martin exclaimed. "I'm an old man with a fine collection of antiques, I have no need to steal!"

"Then what are you doing here?"

"I...I was doing a little investigation. To find out what really happened to Desmond."

It suddenly dawned on Lacey what Martin was actually confessing to. Not to being the thief. Nor the murderer. He was confessing to being an amateur sleuth, just like her. Only the roles were reversed. While she was suspicious of Martin, he was suspicious of her.

She felt a sharp pain in her chest.

"You were investigating me?" she said, taken aback. "You thought I was the killer?"

"I just wanted to make sure you weren't," Martin replied, sounding more polite and formal than ever. "I needed to cross the t's and dot the i's, so to speak. That's all. It was nothing personal."

"Nothing personal?" Lacey repeated incredulously. She couldn't help it. She'd been accused of all sorts of things in her time, but for some reason, this one really stung.

"Were you not investigating me for precisely the same reason?" Martin replied in a haughty tone.

He had her there.

Lacey folded her arms. "Yes. But . . . well . . . I have actual reasons to suspect you."

"More than I do you? An outsider! An antiques expert, no less. One who arrives in town at the same time as a rare gold coin is stolen! Moments before a man is murdered! I think it's plain as day to see how and why my mind went where it did. But for you to suspect me, on the other hand. Well."

He let out an incensed huff. It was the first time Lacey had seen him moved to such a passionate outpouring, and she felt guilty for having caused it.

"You're right," she said, letting her defenses drop at last. "We both had valid reasons to suspect the other."

"What reasons did I give for you to suspect me?" Martin challenged. Lacey might've been able to let her defensiveness go, but Martin evidently had not. "I've lived in Studdleton Bay my whole life! I worked side by side with Desmond years ago! Why would I kill him now?"

"That's what I'm trying to find out," Lacey explained, trying her best to defuse the situation. "If you had nothing to do with anything, then why didn't you mention that you knew the lighthouse I was staying at? You buy your eggs here every week."

Martin frowned. "How do you know that?" Then he let out a deep sigh of realization. "Doris. Of course." He rolled his eyes. "I don't really see how where I buy my eggs has anything to do with anything whatsoever. Would you like to know my brand of detergent? My favorite newspaper? How often I feed the birds? Or if I choose not to divulge to you every passing moment of my life, will that give you a valid reason to point the finger of blame at me!"

Lacey was getting wound up again. She didn't like this side of Martin, even if she had been the one to provoke it.

"It's more than that," she said, irritated, before blurting out, "I know you went to see him the night he died."

Martin fell suddenly very quiet. His pompousness ebbed away. He pressed his lips into a thin line.

"You're right," he said, finally, his tone clipped. "I did go to Forsythe's that night."

Lacey stifled the urge to shout, "A-ha!" Instead, she took the higher ground. "Do you want to tell me why?"

Martin dithered for a moment, then let out a huff like a child who's finally realized there's no way to worm their way out of this one. "When you showed me the coin and said it was from Forsythe's, I was very surprised. Desmond doesn't usually have such high-quality items. I wanted to see if he had any other accidental hidden gems lying around the place." He tipped his gaze to his feet with shame. "I know it was dreadful of me, especially since I'm well aware he only gets his things from swindling elderly people like me."

Lacey thought of the vicar, who Martin had sought out to discuss the moral dilemma over the gold coin with. It hadn't just been her behavior they'd discussed, but also his own.

"Thankfully, the good Lord intervened," Martin added. "When I got to the store, I saw it was quite the opposite..."

Lacey understood what he meant. "The merchandise at Forsythe's was in bad condition and overpriced."

Martin nodded. His voice came out thinly. "And then Desmond died. Do you think it was a punishment for my dishonesty?"

Lacey regarded him once again as the frail old man he really was, rather than the murderer her mind had conjured him to be. She shook her head. "I don't."

"Then who do you think did it?"

Lacey sighed, at loose ends. "I honestly have no idea. But whoever did it, I don't think they were planning on it."

"Oh?" Martin asked. "What makes you say that?"

"The murder weapon was from the store," she said. "A bronze candle holder. It was one of Desmond's swindled pieces that he was trying to sell for more than it was worth. The killer must've grabbed it and struck him in a fit of passion."

"The bronze Rococo in the window?" Martin asked. "Why, anybody could've seen that though. It was on full display."

"I suppose you're right," Lacey said. "If the killer had seen it through the window . . ."

But her voice trailed away as her mind suddenly hit on something.

The killer might well have already known the candle holder was there. Not because they'd seen it through the window, but because they were the one who'd sold it to Desmond in the first place.

"Martin!" she cried, suddenly, grabbing the old man by the hands. "You're a genius!"

She kissed the crown of his head and hurried away, leaving him blinking with bemusement in the dusty farmyard, chickens clucking around his feet.

CHAPTER TWENTY FOUR

Lacey ran out of the Ashworth's farm and onto the road. But she'd barely made it twenty feet when she spotted her family coming up the hill toward her. They must've finished their cocktails at the Cavern and gotten bored of waiting for her so decided to return to the lighthouse. It looked like they'd even managed to squeeze in some shopping in the time she'd been hurrying from the almshouse to the lighthouse, since they were all holding plastic bags.

"It's Auntie Lacey!" Frankie yelled.

They met in the middle of the street.

"Tom's making us fish and potato gratin for dinner," Shirley said.

"Fresh from the mongers," Tom said, holding up a white plastic bag, wafting a distinctly pungent smell her way.

Naomi waved a bottle of fancy-looking wine at her. "We got this from a wine shop. Turns out there are vineyards in the UK. British wine! Who knew?"

"Are you coming with us?" Frankie asked.

"I can't," Lacey said. "I have some stuff to do."

She didn't want to make it too obvious she was still on the hunt for the killer, in case Frankie got any ideas about tagging along. She'd run out of "important tasks" to distract him with, and since the deadline for the fingerprint results was fast approaching, there was no time to waste.

"What stuff?" Tom asked. "Where are you going?" He looked disappointed that she was once again parting ways with the rest of them. His patience for spending time with her family might have finally come to its end. Or perhaps he actually wanted to spend time with her after all?

"I'm sorry," Lacey told him. "But I don't have time to explain."

"You've found a lead, haven't you?" Frankie exclaimed excitedly. "Can I come?"

Tom, who was usually pretty imperceptive, seemed to notice from her expression that Frankie tagging along was not welcome. And though he seemed disappointed that she was rushing off again, he stepped up with a solution.

"I was hoping you'd be my head cook," he said to Frankie.

Frankie turned to Tom, looking proud. "Really? Me?"

Tom nodded. "I thought you might want to learn how to gut a fish?"

Frankie looked thrilled. He turned back to Lacey, his lips twisted. "I'm sorry, Auntie Lacey, but I don't think I can come with you this time."

"That's all right," Lacey said with a nod, before flashing Tom an expression of gratitude. She'd run out of ideas to distract Frankie from danger, but thankfully Tom had stepped in to save the day.

"Whatever you're up to," Tom said to Lacey, taking her in his arms, "please stay safe."

"I will," she replied, before turning and hurrying away.

Thanks to the downward slope of the hills, she got an extra little boost from gravity. She needed all the help she could get. It was getting close to the time the police claimed the fingerprint check would be finished.

When she reached the store she saw the police tape had been cleared away. Inside, the lights were on. Evidently, the meeting with the solicitors had gone without a hitch, and the store's ownership had been transferred from the Studdleton Bay police to Bernadette.

Lacey knocked on the window and sure enough, Bernadette appeared from the back room. She hurried over and unlatched the door.

"You really are keen to get that list of detectorists, huh?" she said. Then she looked either side of Lacey. "What happened to your nephew?"

"Never mind that. I think I might know who killed your uncle."

There was no time for being covert, or coming up with cover stories. She didn't have time for that. Better to just cut to the chase.

Bernadette's expression turned immediately serious. "Oh. Then I suppose you'd better come in."

Lacey didn't need inviting twice. She entered Forsythe's, shutting the door and locking it behind her. Her eyes immediately fell to the stacks of paper on the desk. "Let me guess. That's the itemized stock list from the solicitor?"

"Yup," Bernadette said, following Lacey's glance. "I am now the proud owner of fifty decades' worth of junk." She turned back, a tense expression on her face. "So . . . who do you think killed Uncle Desmond?"

"I'm not one hundred percent sure yet," Lacey said. "That's why I'm here. Can I check through the stock list?"

"Be my guest," Bernadette told her with a shrug. "It's like trying to read a foreign language to me."

Lacey dived right in, scooping up the colorful binders from the counter into her arms.

"Mind if I find somewhere to sit with this?" she asked Bernadette.

"Take the back room," Bernadette said with a shrug. "I'm probably going to be clattering around in here anyway."

She looked around her at the crammed store, looking even more bewildered than she had earlier in the day.

Lacey took the files into the back room of Forsythe's. Like the layout of her own store, the back room was a very large, long room. But unlike her store, where the room was kept relatively empty in order to hold auctions, this one was as busy and full as the main shop floor. Desmond really had amassed a lot of merchandise over the years. No wonder he'd failed to notice the gold coin in the grab bag. Lacey was surprised he'd managed to keep track of anything whatsoever.

She popped herself down onto a small wooden stool that made her think of milking maids, between a stack of superhero magazines from the 1980s and several floor-length mirrors propped against one another. From the other room came the sound of angry metal music. Bernadette had clearly found the sound system.

Lacey got to work, looking through the records Desmond had kept. Contrary to how cluttered his store was, Desmond Forsythe took meticulously neat records. His handwriting was really quite lovely, the type you'd see on greeting cards. All the detectorists' names and addresses were listed, as were the names and addresses of every estate he'd worked on. It was like a rap sheet of swindles, written lovingly in pretty handwriting. And boy was it long! Desmond had made quite the lucrative career out of swindling people.

The first interesting fact was that it didn't look as if Desmond took donations at all. So Angus McRab's story that he'd accidentally donated the gold coin to Desmond in a grab bag fell apart at the first hurdle. There was nothing indicating Desmond had been donated anything from anyone whatsoever. His lists showed he paid for everything (admittedly, too little), but there was no section for donations. At least ninety percent of the grab bags came from detectorists, but there were also entries attributed to the local Bank of Dover. From the information in front of her, it looked as if Desmond bought various assortments of out-of-circulation and commemorative coins. The gold coin wasn't listed anywhere amongst them.

So Angus's story about accidentally donating the gold coin was a load of crock, just as she'd suspected. He was a fraud. How he'd come to know about the gold coin in the first place was still a mystery, though Lacey suspected Doris's gossip was at least partly responsible. The important thing was that Lacey was now completely confident that the gold coin hadn't been Angus's in the first place, and he was just another swindler in this saga.

As Lacey continued searching through the books, she became so absorbed in the task she barely noticed the light outside was starting to fade. Her time was running out fast, and she was still no closer to finding the owner of the candle holder.

She switched folders, swapping the navy blue one with a lime green one. The same cursive writing filled the pages of this book, each one seeming to be a neat record of all the scams Desmond had succeeded in.

Then, suddenly, Lacey found the entry she'd come here for in the first place. Under the section for recent estate sale merchandise purchases, she read: *a pair of bronze Rococo Candle Holders.*

Her heart began to race. This was it. The murder weapon. How odd to think Desmond had penned this entry, not knowing at the time that the item he was listing would be used to end his life.

She scanned through the information to find out where the candle holder had come from. Her eyes settled on the name Jim Swann.

"Jim Swann?" Lacey repeated with a gasp. She knew that name. Where had she heard that before?

Then suddenly, Doris's croaky, shrill voice sounded in her mind. *"She bought the lighthouse after Jimmy Swann died and turned into a B&B of all things! Swindled his family out of a bunch of money too. She and that dead fellow."*

Like a wave breaking on the shore, all the pieces of the puzzle fell into place in Lacey's mind, and she saw with sudden clarity what had happened.

Jimmy Swann was the man who'd owned the lighthouse before Helen. In her words, he'd been using it as "storage." But from the looks of the items that had been purchased by Desmond, the lighthouse was filled with rare antiques and treasures! Had Helen known that when she'd recommended the services of Desmond to Jim Swann's grieving relatives? Or had she only wanted to quickly purchase the lighthouse and turn it into a B&B, and knew getting Desmond involved would be the fastest route to achieving that? Doris had certainly made Helen seem more than complicit in the scam, but Lacey knew from experience not to put too much faith in the accuracy of gossipers. If the Wilfordshire grapevine was to be believed, she was a prolific serial killer.

Still, it was a very interesting find nonetheless, and Lacey quickly looked through the rest of the items that had come from the lighthouse. Jimmy Swann had been in possession of a lot of old, interesting relics when he'd passed. Lacey saw Victorian fringed stand-up lamps in walnut wood, neatly listed beneath an original Aga, a mahogany bureau, a collection of silver serving spoons. They were all items someone like she or Percy would be thrilled to get their hands on, even though they might not fetch a huge sum once they made it to the shop floor. But they were certainly worth more than Desmond had bought them for! Indeed, he'd bought them for pennies on the pound! He'd severely undervalued the contents of Jimmy Swann's lighthouse, and by the figures neatly printed beside each one, those he'd gone on to sell had sold at a huge markup.

Lacey wasn't quite sure what the ten percent figure deducted for Jimmy's page meant, but wondered if it was something to do with inheritance tax, or stamp duty, or some such finickity local Dover specific law she'd not come across in her studies.

She quickly looked through the rest of the details Desmond had jotted down. The contents of the estate had been settled by Jim Swann's son, Walter. The address was written as 8 Station Approach.

Lacey jumped up, excited, and headed back into the main part of the store to tell Bernadette what she'd found. But as she rounded the corner, she stopped dead. Because Bernadette was at the front door of Forsythe's unlocking it in order to allow inside two figures standing the other side of the large glass window. It was detectives Brass and Fryer.

The prints! Lacey thought. They must have gotten their results back early. Her time was up. Her fingerprints would match the pennies found at the crime scene. And worse, she'd known all along that they would. They had come to arrest her.

"Bernadette!" Lacey exclaimed. "Don't—"

But it was too late. Bernadette was already heaving open the large door.

Panicking, Lacey made a sudden, rash decision. She retreated into the back room, bolted for the back exit, and ran.

CHAPTER TWENTY FIVE

"Lacey! Lacey, stop!" Bernadette yelled from behind her.

But Lacey was already streaking down the garden path of Forsythe's. There was no time to stop and gather her thoughts, not with the police after her.

The back garden was about as messy as the main store, filled with a smorgasbord of garden furniture from different cultures and eras, all in the same scruffy state as the merchandise inside, and each with a price tag that far exceeded its worth.

What paltry sum had Desmond paid the grieving relatives of the people these treasures had once belonged to? Lacey thought as she beelined for the back gate.

Just as she reached the gate and stretched forward to unlatch it, she heard the commanding voice of DCI Brass from behind, shouting, "Stop!"

Without hesitating, Lacey heaved open the gate and hurried through. She took a quick glance over her shoulder and saw the two detectives charging down the garden path after her. Bernadette stood fretfully at the back door of Forsythe's, nervously wringing her hands.

Why did she let them in? Lacey thought desperately. Unless, perhaps, she'd been the one to tip them off that Lacey was there. How else would they have known where to find her?

There was no time to work it all out now. The two detectives would be significantly fitter and faster than Lacey, so she had to think of a creative way to lose them, and quick.

She darted into a back alley, where there was a row of garages with painted doors. A group of about ten kids, who looked to be roughly Frankie's age, were running back and forth across the space with a football, using two of the garage doors as goals. A number of them had discarded their bicycles on the ground, and for a brief second, Lacey considered jumping on one and cycling away. But she reminded herself that committing theft in front of two police officers wasn't a good way to convince anyone she was innocent, not to mention the fact that using a bicycle designed for a small child wouldn't get a grown woman very far very fast. She'd be quicker on her feet.

As she got closer to the group of kids, a much better plan suddenly formulated in her mind.

"Over here!" she called to the boy searching for a teammate to pass the ball to.

He dutifully did so, only looking confused once he realized he'd passed the ball to a strange woman who seemed to be joining in with their game of soccer.

As the football rolled to her, Lacey stopped it with her foot, about turned, and kicked it as hard as she could back the way she had come.

"Oops! Sorry!" she called as the kids went charging after it in a chaotic clamor of noise.

She hurried off, letting the group of children run right into the path of the two detectives. Sure, it would only buy her a few extra seconds, but Lacey needed all the help she could get.

If only Chester were here, she thought. He was great at causing a distraction. He'd helped her out of her fair share of sticky situations in the past.

"Watch it!" she heard DCI Brass cry.

Lacey looked back in time to see the detectives trying to shove their way through the mass of kids, then ducked around the side of the garages and out of sight.

She found herself standing on a footpath. If she was lucky, it would be like the footpath that ran around the back of her store in Wilfordshire. That one stretched the entire length of the high street's terrace, with a number of back gates connected to it. If she found a gate that led to the back of a store rather than a property, she may be able to slip inside unnoticed and lose her tail that way.

She ran along, hopping occasionally to peer over the fence. Garden. Garden. Garden. Child bouncing on a trampoline. It seemed as if the footpath was running behind only houses. Lacey didn't want to accidentally commit a misdemeanor while trying to avoid being arrested for a felony!

"There she is!" she heard DCI Fryer's voice call, and looked over to see the two detectives at the far end of the footpath.

"Lacey! Stop!" DCI Brass yelled.

Lacey grabbed the handle of the closest gate, unlatched it, and, uttering a silent prayer that it wouldn't lead her straight into someone's private garden, ran inside.

To her relief, she found herself in what appeared to be the back outside seating area of a cafe. Among the wooden picnic benches sat a couple, who looked at her harried appearance and blinked.

"Just taking a shortcut," Lacey told them, hurriedly, as she weaved through the tables and in through the open back door of the cafe.

"Watch it!" a voice cried.

Lacey had almost walked straight into a waitress carrying two plates of baked potatoes, but luckily they twirled in a strange sort of dance, the waitress lifting the plates above her head, and Lacey was able to slip past without getting a load of coleslaw dumped on her head.

She hurried through the crammed cafe and out through the double glass doors, emerging into the busy smugglers' lanes.

It seemed as if she'd lost her pursuers. But where to now?

Station Approach, Lacey thought. That was the address written beside the bronze candelabra in Desmond's notes. That was where the swindled relatives of Jim Swann lived. And Lacey had a strong hunch that once she found the prior owner of the bronze Rococo candle holder, she'd solve the case.

But the old smugglers' lanes were like a maze. She didn't even know where to start.

Station Approach is probably somewhere near the train station, she told herself. But where was the train station? They'd driven here, and Lacey had hardly had a chance to explore the town since she'd arrived!

She emerged from the alleyway into a pedestrianized square. The architecture here was a mix of old Edwardian, Tudor, and post-war brutalism, a curious mixture that seemed strangely common in the variety of English towns she'd visited. Distant rolling green hills peeped over the tops of the buildings, with imposing, crumbling Norman churches perched on the top them, adding yet another layer of history to the locale. A large water fountain in the middle caught rainbows in its droplets. There were at least five different directions she could now choose, and Lacey found herself turning on the spot desperately searching for a clue that might help her make an informed decision.

Just then, she noticed a group of young people decked out in muddy wellington boots and short, flowery dresses, with ribbons braided into their hair and smudged, faded face paint. They looked suspiciously like they were returning from a summer music festival. If they'd taken the train home, then the path they were coming from may be the one Lacey needed.

"There she is!" cane the sudden voice of DCI Brass.

Lacey ran for the branch, hoping it was the right one, as she squeezed through the group of festival-goers.

"Sorry! Coming through!" she cried.

"Dude, you need to chill out," one of the kids muttered as she hurried past.

The street here narrowed to a single track. The stores were built in Tudor terraces, just like those along Wilfordshire's high street, only they were built much closer together. Awnings covered much of the scant daylight, and Lacey recalled something she'd read in a history book about Tudor's throwing their pots of urine into the streets, the awnings being there to protect the pedestrians passing below. She grimaced, and hastened her pace along the long, dark road.

She passed toy stores and boutiques, gift shops and pubs, hurrying beneath Union Jack flags flapping in the evening breeze. As she ran, she turned to look over her shoulder and caught sight of the two detectives. Dammit! They were still on her tail.

The road began to curve and incline upward.

"Not another hill," Lacey said, panting. She felt like she'd walked up and down about a hundred of them today!

She stopped to catch her breath and collect her thoughts. It didn't make sense to her that the station would be built up a hill. Surely the festival-goers had come from a different route.

She turned on the spot, her gaze passing over the pub on the corner, the random ruins of a church, the parking lot of a leisure center, the overgrown foliage of a roadside hedge, before she suddenly saw a narrow pathway, barely the width of a single person, hidden almost entirely by the buildings it cut between. She hurried to it and, on seeing the light coming from the other end that told her it wasn't a dead end, she rushed along.

At points the path was so narrow her shoulders brushed the walls either side. But when she emerged out the other end—onto a road that looked remarkably similar to the one she'd just left—she discovered she was standing under a tall metal signpost, painted in shiny black paint with its directions written in gold block writing. She scanned the various directions quickly until she saw the symbol of a train.

Her heart leapt.

She rushed off in the direction it was indicating. This time, she began passing more people who'd quite clearly returned from travels elsewhere. There were more festival-goers, and tanned people carrying suitcases who'd quite clearly just returned from a week or two abroad. There were also plenty of people in business clothes, evidently ending a day at the office.

She went against the flow of people, dodging and weaving her way along the sidewalk, until she finally caught sight of the bright red and white sign that showed her she was nearing the station.

"Okay, Station Approach. Station Approach," she said, looking about her for a sign.

Like every other part of Studdleton Bay she'd seen in her hasty jog, there seemed to be roads coming off roads coming off roads. Not a single one had a street sign, which meant any one of them could feasibly be Station Approach!

Then finally, half hidden behind the foliage of an overgrown tree, Lacey saw what she was looking for.

"Station Approach! There it is!"

She hurried onto the road. It looked like something out of a picture book. On either side of the winding street stood three-story terraced town houses, built right next to the sidewalk, without front yards. Thanks to the curve of the street, it looked as if the houses had been squished in together at the strangest of angles, but the yellow-colored stone they were all built from gave the street a sense of unity. Leading up to the brightly painted front doors were several steps, some painted a dark crimson, others tiled with pretty Portuguese-style patterns, others still left in their original slate-gray color. The front doors were all painted in bright colors, with various different styles of door knockers and handles, as if every owner who'd ever lived in the house had left a sign of their personality behind somehow. Some had welcome mats on them, others had Union Jack flags, and others still had baskets of hanging flowers. And to think such a pretty place might well be harboring a murderer!

Now what number? Lacey thought as she hurried along. "Oh yes, eight! The same as Frankie's age!"

The door for number eight was blue and shiny. Eight brick steps led up to it. Lacey ran up them and pounded on the door.

It felt like forever before anything happened. The whole time, Lacey kept glancing over her shoulder anxiously, expecting to see DCI Brass and DCI Fryer suddenly appear.

At last, Lacey heard the sound of the door being opened from inside, and as it was pulled open, a man appeared before her. He looked bewildered to see Lacey standing on his doorstep, panting.

And Lacey, in turn, was just as bewildered to realize she recognized him.

It was the same man she'd seen at the almshouse! The man with the large sweat patches staining the armpits of his white shirt, with the beads of sweat dripping down his troubled face. The man whose appearance had caused the vicar to glare at Doris and stop her loose tongue mid-gossip. Not because he was reminding her not to talk of the dead, Lacey realized, but to remind her not to talk about the dead in front of the very man who'd committed the crime!

Walter Swann had been going to the church to confess his sins!

"Walter Swann?" Lacey asked. "*You're* Walter Swann?"

The man frowned, his bushy white eyebrows drawing together. "Yes. Do I know you?"

But before she could answer, his gaze went over her shoulder.

Lacey turned. A black car came careening around the corner, before halting suddenly. From the passenger side, DCI Fryer leapt out, joined just a moment later by DCI Brass as she emerged from the driver's side. They must've collected their car from near Forsythe's after realizing mid-chase where she was heading, and deciding it was quicker to pursue her that way than on foot.

Lacey gasped and turned back to Walter in his doorway. It was too late. He'd clearly worked out what was going on, that she'd led two plainclothes police detectives right to his doorstep. Now it was his turn to bolt.

He shoved Lacey out of the way. She slammed backwards into the railing, only barely stopping herself from losing her footing and falling down the flight of stairs.

Walter, despite his size, took off down the steps at quite a clip, before reaching the street and bolting off in the opposite direction of the cops.

Now this is getting ridiculous, Lacey thought, as she collected herself from the railings and took off after him. *I'm chasing the actual perp while the police are chasing me because they think I'm the perp!*

"Walter, stop!" she cried at the man's back, which was quickly becoming saturated in his sweat. "It's over! I know what happened!"

Walter wasn't listening.

"Please stop running!" Lacey cried, hearing the footsteps of the two detectives gaining on her, as she, in turn, was gaining on Walter. If the police got to her before she got to him, it would be over and she'd lose the suspect. She was a hair's breadth away from solving this thing! She just had to get him to give up and confess!

Recalling how troubled Walter had looked when she'd seen him at the almshouse, Lacey worked out how she might be able to get a confession out of him. Appeal to his morality. He obviously felt guilt over his actions to be seeking out a vicar.

"I know what Desmond did to you!" she cried. "I know how he swindled your family! How he bought your father Jim's entire estate for a pittance, then sold it on for profit!"

Her voice seemed to bounce from one side of the street to the other, echoing between the terraced houses. More than a few curtains started twitching as the neighbors were alerted to the ruckus taking place outside their homes.

"I know you never meant to hurt him!" Lacey cried at Walter's back. "You didn't go over there intending to kill him. But something happened once you got there." She thought of the sneering Desmond, of how he'd so quickly insulted her and Frankie, how he'd yelled at her, how he had no friends and a whole lot of enemies. Desmond must have said something to Walter to provoke his violent response. "You just happened to be holding the candelabra at the time, didn't you? You found out about the swindle and went over there to confront him. Picked up the candle holder to show him. And then he said something and you snapped. You hit him over the head with the overpriced candle holder he'd swindled off you in the first place!"

All at once, the man slowed from a run to a trot. Then he stopped completely, bent forward, and put his hands on his knees. Lacey couldn't tell whether he'd just run out of breath, or if her appeal had made him decide to give up the chase. Whichever it was, it didn't matter to Lacey. She jogged up to Walter's side just as DCI Brass and Fryer caught up with her.

"Police!" DCI Brass cried, panting. "Everyone stop what you're doing!"

Lacey stood in the middle of the quaint Studdleton Bay street, her hands in the air. She kept one eye on Walter Swann in case he decided to bolt again, and one of the two plainclothes police officers approaching her with their handcuffs at the ready.

"Did you hear what I said?" she said as they drew ever closer. "About the candlestick and the swindle?"

"We heard," DCI Brass said. "The whole street heard."

Lacey saw the curtains twitch in the cottage ahead of her.

"Then why are you arresting me?" she pleaded.

"We're not," DCI Brass said. "So you can put your hands down."

Lacey hesitated. "You're not?"

"No. We're arresting him!"

"What?" Lacey said, lowering her hands. "But the prints..."

"Weren't a match for you," DCI Brass finished for her, passing her and walking up to Walter. She cuffed him. "They matched Desmond's prints, and no one else's."

"But then, no one was framing me for Desmond's murder?" Lacey stammered.

"Doesn't look that way," DCI Brass said, in her dispassionate way.

Lacey didn't understand. She looked back and forth at everyone. "Why were you coming to the shop if not to arrest me? And why were you chasing me through the streets?"

"We'd already flagged that whoever Desmond had bought the candle holder from was likely the killer," DCI Brass said. "We went to the shop to see whether we could find out the name and address of the prior owner in the records. Turns out we just had to follow you."

Fryer clapped her on the back. "You did a good investigation, Lacey."

It was far from how Superintendent Turner would have treated her. Lacey couldn't help but smile with pride.

As DCI Brass began leading Walter Swann back toward the car, he gave Lacey a long look. She saw no malice in his eyes. In fact, she saw relief. Relief that his burden had finally been lifted, that he no longer had to carry his guilty secret.

"Come on, let's head back to the station," DCI Brass said to Lacey. "I think we all need to have a little chat."

Lacey took a sip of her watery vending machine coffee, hearing the click of the handle as the door to the questioning room was opened.

DCI Fryer walked in, manila folder in hand. He slapped it down onto the table with triumph. "He confessed to everything," he announced. "The whole thing."

Lacey was so relieved she could have hugged him. "So what happened?"

"It was pretty much how you pictured it," Sebastian Fryer said, taking the seat next to her. "He found out Desmond had swindled him when he saw a pair of Rococo candle holders for sale online for a grand. Desmond had paid him ten pounds for the pair. He went over to confront him, seeing that the candle holder was in the window priced at three grand, knowing Desmond was going to swindle not just him, but the person who bought them. He snapped."

Lacey whistled.

"We got some CCTV footage of him near the crime scene around the time of death on the autopsy reports, and a witness statement, who claimed to have heard an argument erupting in the store over the price of a candle holder. Add all that to the confession, and the testimony of a local vicar Walter spoke to in a state and I'd say we have a pretty ironclad case to take to the prosecutor's office."

"Sounds like a home run for you guys," Lacey said.

She felt her cheeks growing warm with embarrassment. She'd completely misunderstood the situation by thinking they'd made her the prime suspect. Clearly the Studdleton Bay police were a bit more switched on than the Wilfordshire police!

"I'm sorry if I stepped on your toes at any point," she said. "I guess I was never a suspect after all."

"Oh, you were a suspect," came the voice of DCI Brass from the doorway behind. Lacey turned as the female officer entered the small room, watching her walk over and take the seat opposite. "You made yourself one by getting overly involved in our investigation, and you stayed as one right up until the fingerprint results came back from the archaeologist's."

"The prints on the coins!" Lacey exclaimed. "That's the bit I don't understand. I was sure someone was trying to frame me."

"That was actually a coincidence," DCI Fryer said. "Or, perhaps, a coincidence." He smiled at his own joke.

DCI Brass took up the explanation. "According to Walter, when he went to the store to challenge Desmond over being scammed, the man showed him some pennies and said that was all the extra he would give. That, apparently, was the moment he snapped. The pennies fell from Desmond's hand into the armchair as he sunk into it and died."

"So they weren't stolen from my room," Lacey said. She knew Frankie had been overconfident about his knot skills. The grab bag had fallen from its perch in the trunk of the elephant figurine and spilled across the shelf after all.

"Stolen?" DCI Brass said, looking interested. "From your room?"

Lacey waved it away with a hand. "Yes. Just a mistake. My nephew thought someone had broken into our room at the lighthouse inn and stolen some of his Roman coins from the grab bag. But nothing else was stolen and there was no sign of a break-in, so I think he was just getting caught up in his imagination. He has quite a creative mind."

The two detectives exchanged a glance.

"You're staying at the lighthouse inn?" DCI Fryer asked.

For some reason, Lacey's mention of the theft at the inn had piqued the two detectives' interest. But then again, it was their job to be curious, Lacey reasoned.

"Honestly, it's nothing," she assured them. "Just a misunderstanding."

"Maybe," DCI Brass said. "But maybe not. That's the second report we've had regarding a theft at the lighthouse inn."

Lacey blink with surprise. "Really?"

DCI Fryer nodded. "Our last case was going cold. We'd run out of leads. Do you mind if we come over and take a look?"

"Sure," Lacey said with a shrug. "If you're lucky, there might just be some freshly cooked fish gratin in it for you as well."

CHAPTER TWENTY SIX

"Would you like some wine, Sebastian?" Naomi said, gesturing with the bottle toward DCI Fryer.

"No thank you," the detective said, so clearly intimidated by her presence he couldn't even take his eyes off the elephant figurine he was dusting for prints. "Not while I'm on duty."

"What about when you're off duty?" Naomi purred.

Lacey caught Tom's eye and stifled her giggle.

The two detectives had driven to the lighthouse with Lacey, intruding on the middle of the fish gratin supper. Which had immediately caused Frankie to accost them with a million and one questions, Shirley to accost them with offers of food, and Naomi to accost DCI Fryer specifically with her flirting attempts.

Frankie sat on the couch as DCI Brass finished taking his statement about how he'd found the grab bag untied.

"What happens to the gold coin now?" Frankie asked DCI Brass as he took a bite of his dessert from the bowl perched on his knees—a bread pudding Tom had made, swimming in custard. "Does it belong to Bernadette Forsythe or to Walter Swann? If Walter accidentally sold it to Desmond along with all of his dad's items, but Desmond didn't even know it was there and didn't log it in his inventory, then whose is it? Who do we give it to? Who gets to ride the Jacobite Steam Train through the Highlands?"

"It won't go to Walter Swann," DCI Brass explained calmly. "Because he's in jail. So if it's listed as one of Desmond's possessions, it will go to his niece."

"And if it's not?"

"Then there's a chance it will be yours. But I shouldn't spend any of it just in case."

Frankie nodded. He seemed satisfied with that explanation.

DCI Brass stood. "I think we're all done here. Fryer?"

The male detective stood, too, and stepped back when he realized Naomi was hovering barely an inch away from him.

"All done," he said, slipping off his latex gloves.

"That's a shame," Naomi said. "It was fun having a handsome man in the house."

Frankie stuck out his tongue with disgust. Shirley rolled her eyes.

"We'll be in touch," DCI Brass said as she headed for the spiral staircase.

"Enjoy the rest of your vacation," DCI Fryer added.

"How about you call me when your shift is over?" Naomi called after him. Her question was met by silence.

Lacey listened for the sound of the door closing before she burst out laughing. "Naomi! You're shameless!"

"What?" her sister said, defensively. "He was cute."

"He was half a foot shorter than you."

"So? He's still a catch. Besides, being with a Brit worked out so well for you."

Lacey looked over at Tom and slid her arm around his waist. "You're right. It did work out well for me." She pecked him on the lips.

"Ew!" Frankie cried.

Bernadette let out a low exhalation. Her hands were clasped around an energy drink. "So that's how it happened, huh?"

Lacey nodded slowly and leaned back in the chair. "Yeah. I thought you'd want to know."

She'd just visited Forsythe's to give Bernadette the lowdown on her uncle's murder, knowing the police would have to err on the side of caution until they explained the situation.

"Thanks," Bernadette said. She took a swig of energy drink. "I know my uncle wasn't the best guy in the world, but he didn't deserve to die for it. That really sucks."

"It does," Lacey said with a gentle nod. "I'm really sorry."

Bernadette shrugged. "Hey, well, you know you did everything you could to help. So thanks. Actually, I wanted to give you something."

"You did?" Lacey asked, surprised.

Bernadette nodded and stood from the chair, placing her energy drink on the antique Victorian nested side table—which Lacey promptly removed and wiped the surface of with her sleeve—before disappearing into the back room. She reemerged a moment later holding a small parcel wrapped in newspaper and tied with string.

"I didn't have any wrapping paper on hand," Bernadette said as she handed the package to Lacey.

But Lacey was so touched, she didn't care about that at all. "This is so kind of you. Shall I open it now?"

Bernadette nodded.

Lacey carefully untied the string and removed the newspaper. In her hands, she was holding a small red leather book, very worn and dog-eared from years of use. The gold lettering on its front was faded, and Lacey had to squint.

"Oh!" she exclaimed. "It's a copy of *The Canterbury Tales*."

The name of the town her father had potentially been traced to made her heart skip a beat.

"You said you know the town," Bernadette said.

Lacey nodded, too taken aback to say anything yet. It felt like some kind of a sign. That Bernadette was a student at Canterbury, and had thought to gift her this novel, it all seemed like the universe telling her something.

"I never asked how you knew the university, though," Bernadette said.

"It's a long story," Lacey told her. She clutched the book like it was a lifeline. "Thank you for this. Truly. It means more than you know. But I really don't know what I did to deserve it."

"Actually . . ." Bernadette began. "It's kind of a preemptive thank you." She scratched the shaved bit of her hair, looking uncomfortable. "I kinda need your help."

"Oh?"

"You see, I don't think I can keep the store open," Bernadette confessed. "It's just I'm right in the middle of my degree and I just have no interest in it. When we were reading through those books together, it just seemed like gobble-dygook. But you read all that stuff like it was your native language! So . . . I guess what I'm trying to ask is, will you help me value everything in the store properly so I can sell it on?"

"Me?" Lacey asked, surprised and touched. "But what about Martin Ormsby?"

"Martin Ormsby wanted to see if my uncle had any more accidental gold coins hidden in any of the other grab bags," she said, disdainfully. "Whereas you came to the store to return the coin. So, I guess what I'm saying is, I trust you more."

Lacey was extremely touched. Percy had been the one to help her, and it was about time she passed on the favor to someone else. It was in the antiquers' play book after all, and if she didn't help out, she'd be one step closer to becoming like Desmond.

"I'd be honored," she told the young woman.

"Really?" Bernadette gushed, looking suddenly relieved. She grabbed Lacey's hand. "Thank you so much! That's such a weight off my mind. And once it's all valued, can you recommend an auctioneer for it all?"

"Funny you should say that," Lacey told her. "I have a little bit of auction-eering experience myself. We could sell the stuff in my auction room back in Wilfordshire, once you're ready."

"You're a lifesaver!" Bernadette said. "My dad is going to be so surprised when he finds out I've organized all this on my own."

She looked proud. She'd come to Studdleton Bay a bewildered girl, and was leaving an accomplished woman. Lacey smiled, glad for the small part she'd played in Bernadette's journey.

"I'd better go," Lacey said. "We're heading home today."

She stood. The young woman did too. Then she suddenly embraced her.

"Oh!" Lacey exclaimed, surprised.

"Thank you, Lacey," Bernadette said. "Speak soon?"

"You bet," Lacey said. "Good luck with your studies."

Lacey headed out of Forsythe's, giving a final wave to Bernadette.

It was finally time to leave Studdleton Bay and Lacey didn't mind admitting, she was relieved to be going home. As her family tried to repack their now overstuffed cases, Lacey sat out in the farmyard with the chickens, soaking up some of the warm summer sunshine she'd barely had a chance to enjoy. She hadn't bought anything during the trip, so her case was already packed.

"Lacey?" Tom called, as he crossed the yard with their suitcases, ready to load into the car. "Did you hand the keys back to Helen yet?"

"I'll do it now," Lacey said.

Just then, Frankie skipped out of the lighthouse up to Lacey's side. "Can I come with you? I want to pet Swuddly one last time."

"Who?"

"The calico cat," he said. "He looked so sweet and cuddly, I called him Swuddly."

"Naturally," Lacey quipped. She ruffled Frankie's hair, amused by his inventive brain. "That's quite the name."

"That's just his nickname," Frankie added. "His full name is Swuddlington Snugglesby. Swuddly for short."

Lacey just laughed. What on earth went on in that mind of his?

She and her partner in crime crossed the dusty farmyard toward Helen's bright red cow shed.

"Hey, look," Frankie said as they walked. "The Scottish guy from the Bluebird Inn was the other guest all along!"

Lacey turned. Emerging from the lighthouse carrying a bag and dragging a suitcase was the unmistakable bulking figure of Angus McRab.

"That's the man from the restaurant?" Lacey stammered. "But it's Angus McRab!"

"The museum man?" Frankie exclaimed.

"And he was the guest on the bottom floor all along."

So that's how he'd found out about the coin! He'd overheard her and Frankie talking about it in their loud American voices.

Behind Angus followed a woman wearing dark sunglasses. She was about half his size in stature, but her scowl was just as mean and brooding as his.

"That must be the wife," Lacey said out of the side of her mouth to Frankie.

Just then, Angus noticed the pair of them in the farmyard. He glared at them darkly and said something to his wife. Her gaze snapped to them and glowered.

"You!" she screamed. "You're the one who stole my coin!"

The pair of them came marching toward them, kicking the chickens out of their path boorishly.

Lacey didn't like where this was going. When it had been just her versus Angus, he'd been ready to get physical. Now that there were two of them, she was even more worried.

She looked around for an escape route, but there was nowhere to run. Her instinct was to protect Frankie, and so she shoved him behind her and braced herself for whatever Angus and his horrible wife were about to throw at her.

"Hey!" Naomi suddenly screeched from the door of the lighthouse. On seeing her son in peril, she did what any mother would do, dropped her arm full of shopping bags and came pelting across the farmyard yelling bloody murder.

Naomi was still halfway across the yard when Angus, just an inch from striking Lacey, was halted in his tracks by the sudden shrill blaring of a police siren.

A police car came careening into the farmyard and screeched to a halt. DCI Fryer leapt out of the passenger seat. He slid across the hood of the car, landing squarely on both feet, and tackled Angus to the ground.

Naomi reached them, pulling Frankie into her arms. "My baby. My baby. Are you okay?"

"Did you SEE that, Mom?" Frankie cried, pointing at where DCI Fryer was grappling Angus to the ground and cuffing him.

Naomi looked over. "I saw it, all right," she gushed.

The driver's door opened to the cruiser and DCI Brass got out. She came to Lacey's side. Lacey's heart was still racing like a jackhammer.

"Are you guys mind readers or something?" Lacey asked the female detective, as her male counterpart finally managed to heave the cuffed Angus up to his feet. "How did you know Angus was going to attack me?"

"Actually, we weren't here for him," DCI Brass said.

"Then why are you here?" Lacey asked. "I'm assuming it's not to buy organic eggs, since you came careening around the corner with your lights flashing and sirens blaring."

"That was Fryer's doing," DCI Brass said with an eye roll. "The second he sees a damsel in distress he goes into hero mode."

Naomi, realizing she was the damsel in distress, smiled.

Lacey glanced over at the cruiser. Angus was glowering angrily in the back seat, while Naomi twirled her hair in her fingers and complimented DCI Fryer on his tackling skills.

"We were actually here to speak to Helen," DCI Brass continued. "About the thefts at the inn."

"Oh yes, did the fingerprints on the elephant figurine yield anything interesting?" Lacey asked.

"Yes and no," DCI Brass explained. "The only prints we lifted were Helen's."

"Makes sense, since she owns the place," Lacey said. "So that explains the 'no.' But what's the 'yes' for?"

"Because the *only* prints we found were Helen's," DCI Brass repeated, only this time with added emphasis.

"Wait . . ." Lacey said, as it started to dawn on her.

DCI Brass nodded. "No one else went into your room. It was Helen who was rifling through your belongings. Hence the lack of any sign of a break-in."

"But why?" Lacey exclaimed.

"Turns out she was working with Desmond. After she helped him swindle the Swanns out of their inheritance."

Lacey's mouth dropped open. She hadn't been sure before how much Helen had really known about what Desmond was getting up to. She'd assumed Helen knew something dodgy was going on, but chose to turn a blind eye because of how she wanted to get her hands on the lighthouse. But by what DCI Brass was telling her, it seemed as if she'd acted as Desmond's righthand man! Or woman!

"Took ten percent for every recommendation," DCI Brass added.

That's what the ten percent deduction figure had been for in Jim Swann's records. It was the cream Helen was skimming off the top!

"We were looking through Desmond's records," the detective continued. "The stolen goods were listed right there in Helen's neat writing."

The writing. Of course. It had looked feminine because it was feminine. Helen had been the one keeping the records.

"So you're arresting her for being a part of the scam?" Lacey asked.

DCI Brass shook her head. "Actually, nothing she and Desmond did was technically illegal. Immoral, yes. But illegal, no. And we don't have enough evidence to arrest her for the theft. So we thought we'd put a bit of pressure on her and see if she confesses voluntarily, a la Walter Swann."

Lacey recalled the way the woman often watched her through the windows before darting back into the shadows. She was nervous. And if she was that nervous around Lacey, she'd probably fall to pieces in front of the cops.

DCI Fryer came over to DCI Brass, Naomi trotting behind him like a lamb.

"Ready for arrest number two?" he said in an uncharacteristically suave voice.

"Let's not get too ahead of ourselves, Romeo," DCI Brass quipped, slapping him on the back.

They headed off into the barn.

Naomi rested her head on Lacey's shoulder. "Well, that was exciting, wasn't it?"

Lacey chuckled. "See, I told you living in England was interesting."

Tom and Shirley came out of the lighthouse then. They exchanged a perplexed glance, first at the sight of the police cruiser with its light still flashing, then the scowling "museum man" who was cuffed in the back seat, then the feathers fluttering all over the farmyard, before finally looking at the two sisters arm in arm.

"What happened here?" Shirley asked.

Frankie immediately jumped in. "Grandma! You should've seen it! It was SO cool!"

He took Shirley's hand, talking her through the story as they walked over to the Volvo together, Naomi in tow.

"You okay?" Tom asked Lacey.

She kissed him tenderly. "I've never been better."

"Great. Well, shall we get out of here?"

Lacey smiled. "Yes. Let's go home."

EPILOGUE

In the middle of the airport concourse, Lacey hugged Naomi tightly. "Enjoy your time in Edinburgh," she said. She heard her sister sniff loudly and drew back. "Naomi, are you crying?"

Naomi dabbed away her tears. "Of course I'm crying, dummy! I'm going to miss you."

Lacey was touched. When she'd rushed away from New York City, she'd been thinking of everything she was running from—David, Saskia, her job—rather than everyone she was leaving behind—her mom, Naomi, and Frankie. Their visit had put things back into perspective, and Lacey felt a bit guilty about it all.

Lacey hugged Shirley next. Her time with her mom had also been transformative. Seeing her mom stand up for her against Angus McRab in the museum had been a bonding moment, one they both desperately needed. And her mother seemed to adore Tom, to the extent where Lacey could actually picture her one day accepting that David was in the past, and any hope of him becoming her son-in-law again and father to her grandchildren was out of the question. Perhaps one day, Shirley may even accept Lacey was working in antiques like her father. Perhaps, even, they may one day be able to mention Frank's name without setting off the atomic bomb of emotions.

"Bye, Mom," Lacey said. "Thank you for coming."

Shirley pressed a hand to her daughter's cheek. "I'm proud of you, sweetheart."

Frankie suddenly flung his arms around Lacey's waist, squeezing her in his aggressively affectionate way. Lacey immediately felt emotion rise in her throat. She was going to miss the silly ginger goofball like crazy. He'd been the best sidekick she could've hoped for.

"Have the best time in Scotland," she told him, squeezing tightly. "Send me a million pictures. And try haggis. And then send me pictures of you trying haggis."

Frankie laughed and let go. "Okay, Auntie Sherlock. See you next adventure."

Her family lifted their cases and waved as they crossed the concourse to the gate. Lacey rested her head on Tom's shoulder, feeling a combination of sadness and relief. She loved her family, but boy were they hard work.

"Ready?" Tom asked, rubbing her arm affectionately.

Lacey nodded.

They headed out of the airport and walked back to the car. But just before Lacey opened the door, her pocket started vibrating with an incoming call on her cell phone. She fished it out. It was the Wilfordshire Veterinarian calling.

Lacey went into an immediate panic. Chester had only been at the vet's for the long weekend. Lakshmi had predicted a two-week stay. Something must've happened.

She pressed the green button. "Lakshmi? What's wrong? What's happened to Chester?"

The voice on the other end of the line was reassuring. "Nothing. He's absolutely fine. That's what I was calling to tell you. You can come and collect him whenever you're ready."

Lacey's heart soared. "Really? But how? I thought he'd be in for at least a fortnight!" She held her hand over the mouthpiece and mouthed to the troubled-looking Tom, "He's fine."

On the other end of the line, Lakshmi continued. "Turns out he actually had a case of acute infectious tracheobronchitis."

"What's that?"

"Bronchitis. And it cleared up quickly. So, he's ready to come home."

Lacey could've punched the air, she was so happy. She'd missed her canine companion more than words could say.

"We're on our way."

Lakshmi the vet was smiling widely as she entered the reception room holding a leash. "Here he is!" she exclaimed. "Right as rain."

Chester trotted into the reception area of the veterinary looking like the healthy, happy dog he always was. The second he caught sight of Tom and Lacey, he looked like all his Christmases had come at once and started whining loudly and straining at his leash.

Lacey crouched, her eyes flooding with tears, and held her arms out to him. "Come here, boy."

Lakshmi walked him over and Chester pounced at Lacey hard enough to knock her onto her behind. But she didn't care. She ruffled his fur and velvety ears, and nuzzled him as enthusiastically as he nuzzled her. She didn't care about the judgmental cat watching on from its basket beside them, nor its equally judgmental-looking owner!

Tom took the leash from Lakshmi. "Thanks for taking such good care of him."

"Oh, he was a pleasure," Lakshmi told them. "And besides, Gina was here chatting with him half the time. She's a hoot and a half."

"She really is," Tom said.

"I'm going to have to get her a huge present," Lacey said. "She does so much for me. I'd be lost without that woman."

They thanked Lakshmi again for everything and headed to the car.

It had been a really long day and Lacey was exhausted. But it was almost over. They were almost back at Crag Cottage.

They got inside the car, and Chester curled up in the backseat. As Lacey turned the ignition and the old secondhand car spluttered to life, Tom touched her hand lightly.

"I'm sorry the trip wasn't what you were expecting," he told her, with a wry look.

"It's not your fault Desmond got killed," she told him.

"Not that," he said. "I mean about your family tagging along. That was my fault. I just didn't know what else to do. I didn't think it would be fair to just leave them here when they'd flown all the way from New York City to see you and I didn't realize it would be so trying for you. I mean, I should've realized since you've told me a million times but I guess I...well...I also was sort of relieved for the distraction."

Lacey's brow furrowed. Tom was babbling. It wasn't like him to be nervous. What was going on?

"What did you need distracting from?" she asked, feeling her stomach start to fall. "From me?"

"No," he said. "Well, sort of."

Lacey felt a pit opening up inside of her. Was Tom ending things? Had her crazy family scared him away? Or worse . . . had she?

"I'm getting this all wrong . . ." Tom said, scratching his neck awkwardly.

"Just get it over with," Lacey said, exhaling sadly.

"What I'm trying to say," Tom said, "is that I timed the trip for our three-month anniversary because I wanted to tell you that . . . that I love you."

Lacey's eyebrows shot up. That was not what she'd been expecting.

"You *love* me?" she stammered.

Tom looked flustered like she'd never seen him. "Yes. I had this whole thing planned, you know, with all the photo clues, and then there was going to be a final one to send you once we were at the restaurant and then I started getting nervous because I thought maybe it was too soon, and when your family turned up I decided it was probably a sign that it *was* too soon so . . ."

Lacey reached out her hand and gently touched his jaw. His nervous babbling ceased

"It's not too soon," she said, tenderly. "I love you too."

"Oh." Tom let out a huge breath. Then he grinned his gorgeous grin. "Well, that's a relief."

He leaned over to her and kissed her passionately.

From the backseat, Chester whined.

"All right!" Lacey said, releasing Tom. "We're going."

She pulled out of the vet's parking lot, recalling Frankie calling it the *carrr parrrk*, and onto the streets that led toward the cliffsides. As she went, her cell started ringing.

"It's a Dover number," Tom said, looking at the screen.

"Who could it be?" Lacey asked. The only people in Dover who had her telephone number were the Studdleton Bay police, Helen Ashworth, and Bernadette. Anxiety swirled in her stomach.

"I'll find out," Tom said, answering her cell for her.

Lacey listened to his half of the conversation as she turned onto the final cliffside road that led to Crag Cottage. She pulled into the parking area just as Tom finished the call.

"So?" she asked. "What did they want?"

"That was Joanne from the police station," he said. "Calling about the evidence."

Lacey thought of the pink-shirted woman in the courtyard who'd arranged for the fingerprint test for DCI Brass.

"What evidence?" she asked. "You mean the Roman pennies?"

"No. The gold coin."

"What about it?"

"It's yours."

Lacey's eyes widened. "What?"

"Bernadette's lawyer confirmed it wasn't part of Desmond's estate, and that there was a receipt as proof of purchase for the grab bag you bought it in. So it's officially yours. Bernadette isn't contesting it. Walter can't. So it's yours."

Lacey's mouth dropped open. She didn't know what to say. The coin could sell for hundreds of thousands of pounds. "Frankie can go on the Jacobite Steam Train..." was all she managed.

"Or," Tom said, laughing heartily, opening the passenger side door, "you could start a college fund for him. He's obviously extremely bright."

"That's a much more sensible idea," Lacey said, laughing in reply. She got out of the driver's seat and reached into the back to collect her bags. "I could put half the money from its sale away for Frankie, and use the other half on the store. And get a big gift for Gina!"

Chester woke up from where he'd been snoozing in the back seat and leapt into Tom's vacant seat, then out through his door. He knocked something on the way, and it hit the gravel with a crunch.

"What's this?" Tom asked, leaning down to pick it up.

It was the copy of *The Canterbury Tales* that Bernadette had given her. Lacey had put it in the side pouch and Chester must have dislodged it as he'd leapt out of the car.

"Oh. It was a gift from Bernadette," Lacey said. "Want me to read to you?"

Tom chuckled. "That sounds relaxing."

They carried their bags into Crag Cottage and slumped down onto the couch together. Lacey was exhausted from the long day. Tom snuggled into her on one side, Chester on the other. It was about as cozy as she could possibly be.

Lacey opened the red leather hardback cover. "There's an inscription inside," she said, before clearing her throat and reading aloud, "*My love. I will always remember the day we met in Wilfordshire* . . . Wilfordshire!" she exclaimed. "What are the chances?" She continued reading, "*I will always be in Canterbury, waiting for you, if you ever change your mind.*" Her voice grew thinner and smaller as she went on reading, until the last sentence came out as barely a whisper. "*All my love, Frank.*"

Lacey went cold all over. Frank. Her father's name. Wilfordshire, the town he took them to on vacation. Canterbury, the place Xavier had supposedly tracked him to.

"Tom," Lacey stammered.

Tom jerked up. He'd evidently fallen asleep the second she began speaking and hadn't heard a word she'd said.

"What is it?" he asked, panicked. "What's wrong? What's happened?" He grabbed her hands.

Lacey stared into his eyes. "Tom. I think I found my dad."

Now Available for Pre-Order!

KILLED WITH A KISS
(A Lacey Doyle Cozy Mystery–Book 5)

"Very entertaining. I highly recommend this book to the permanent library of any reader that appreciates a very well written mystery, with some twists and an intelligent plot. You will not be disappointed. Excellent way to spend a cold weekend!"

　　—Books and Movie Reviews, Roberto Mattos (regarding *Murder in the Manor*)

KILLED WITH A KISS (A LACEY DOYLE COZY MYSTERY—BOOK 5) is book five in a charming new cozy mystery series which begins with MURDER IN THE MANOR (Book #1), a #1 Bestseller with over 100 five-star reviews—and a free download!

Lacey Doyle, 39 years old and freshly divorced, has made a drastic change: she has walked away from the fast life of New York City and settled down in the quaint English seaside town of Wilfordshire.

In a romantic daytrip in the English countryside, Lacey lucks out in an antique market and stumbles upon an incredible find. She has high hopes as she makes it the centerpiece of her next auction.

But as summer is coming to a close, two high-rollers come into town and duke it out over the antique, their egos as big as their wallets. When one of them wins but loses the auction on a technicality, chaos ensues. The only thing that makes it worse is when one ends up dead.

Lacey finds herself in the fight of her life to save her business and her reputation—and, with the help of her beloved dog, to solve the mysterious death.

Book #6 in the series will be available soon!

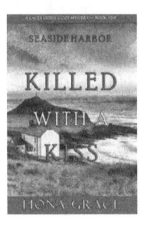

KILLED WITH A KISS
(A Lacey Doyle Cozy Mystery—Book 5)

ALSO NOW AVAILABLE FOR PRE-ORDER!
A NEW SERIES!

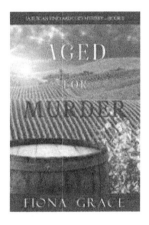

AGED FOR MURDER
(A Tuscan Vineyard Cozy Mystery—Book 1)

"Very entertaining. I highly recommend this book to the permanent library of any reader that appreciates a very well written mystery, with some twists and an intelligent plot. You will not be disappointed. Excellent way to spend a cold weekend!"

　—Books and Movie Reviews, Roberto Mattos (regarding *Murder in the Manor*)

AGED FOR MURDER (A TUSCAN VINEYARD COZY MYSTERY) is the debut novel in a charming new cozy mystery series by #1 bestselling author Fiona Grace, author of Murder in the Manor (Book #1), a #1 Bestseller with over 100 five-star reviews—and a free download!

When Olivia Glass, 34, concocts an ad for a cheap wine that propels her advertising company to the top, she is ashamed by her own work—yet offered the promotion she's dreamed of. Olivia, at a crossroads, realizes this is not the life she signed up for. Worse, when Olivia discovers her long-time boyfriend, about to propose, has been cheating on her, she realizes it's time for a major life change.

Olivia has always dreamed of moving to Tuscany, living a simple life, and starting her own vineyard.

When her long-time friend messages her about a Tuscan cottage available, Olivia can't help wonder: is it fate?

Hilarious, packed with travel, food, wine, twists and turns, romance and her newfound animal friend—and centering around a baffling small-town murder that Olivia must solve—AGED FOR DEATH is an un-putdownable cozy that will keep you laughing late into the night.

Books #2 and #3 in the series—AGED FOR DEATH and AGED FOR MAYHEM—are now also available!

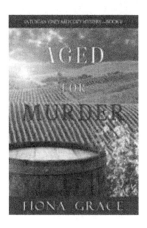

AGED FOR MURDER
(A Tuscan Vineyard Cozy Mystery–Book 1)

Made in the USA
Las Vegas, NV
13 March 2024

87155721R00114